I0709180

CRACKING THE SPINE

ten short Australian stories
and how they were written

Edited by

Julie Chevalier and Bronwyn Mehan

SPINELESS WONDERS

SPINELESS WONDERS

ABN 98156041888

PO Box 220 STRAWBERRY HILLS

New South Wales, Australia, 2012

www.shortaustralianstories.com.au

Cracking the Spine first published by Spineless Wonders 2014

Cover design by Bettina Kaiser, bettinakaiser.com

Cover photo: *Tathra Nude #1* by Anna Brown, blackboxwhitecube.com.au

Layout by Bronwyn Mehan

Photo Credits: Ryan O'Neill p2, Claire Aman p48, Tony Birch p64,
Michael Giacometti p80, Blushnewmedi, via Pinterest, Creative Commons p94,
John Gaydon, steamtrainstories.com.au p116,
joiseyshowaa via Flickr, Creative Commons p126, Patrick West p144,
Tormod Sandorv via Flickr, Creative Commons p164.

Typeset in Adobe Garamond Pro

Printed and bound by Lightning Source Australia

National Library of Australia Cataloguing-in-Publication entry

Cracking the Spine/Eds Julie Chevalier and Bronwyn Mehan

1st ed.

978-1-925052-03-9 (pbk.)

808.3

This project has been assisted by the Australian Government through the Australia Council, its arts funding and advisory body.

'Writers write. You meet them in their books.
Any time you want to.'

Michael Wilding

CONTENTS

INTRODUCTION

A short story is a minefield. So much compressed into so little space. So much of it below the surface.

Some years ago I judged a short story competition that offered substantial prize money. There were over four hundred entries and during the reading process the three judges had no communication. When finally we conferred to make our decision we discovered we had all picked the same winner. What odds? Well, you are thinking, a good story will stand out, will be self-selecting. But not so. In another competition I read for, again as one of three judges, again offering a big prize, the judges disagreed. About halfway through my reading of the entries I came to a story that took my breath away. It was artfully structured, though not in any obvious way. The main characters were established with an immediate presence and with their own distinctively nuanced voices. The dialogue was subtle but revealing. The development when it came surprised me but, like all good plot development, seemed inevitable once it arrived. And, in the narratological equivalent of the quadruple somersault and pike, the very last sentence of the story recast its entire meaning, not in a facile or programmatic way but with uncanny deftness and authority. I could almost hear the click as the structure fell into place. That story had something rare, a formal beauty. It also moved me.

Full of enthusiasm I turned up at the judges' meeting to find my two colleagues had chosen another story. That story had no development, no structure, no characters as such but it did have some pretty writing of the kind described as poetic. I objected. This story is only a vignette, I argued. But the writer has a gift for metaphor, came the reply. Yes, but nothing happens, and it rambles. Ah, but it's exquisitely written. And so on. We debated form. We debated the short story as an art. I lost.

I've kept copies of the best stories from both competitions. Every year they prompt me to re-read them. A good story never leaves you. It enlarges the space in your head.

I still get into arguments about form, and my breathing is often the most reliable test of whether a story is working. If I'm holding my breath then something is at stake.

We can get technical. We can discuss the art and the craft of the story but the primal thing is the voice. Is it arresting or seductive? Do I want to listen to this voice? Does it stop me in my tracks and induce me to put all else aside? Am I captured? When I browse in a bookshop, initially I may be drawn by good reviews, or by subject matter but then I apply the flick-through test. I open the book at random and I am looking to see, and hear, if the voice is there for me, if it compels my attention. Sometimes I think in terms not of favourite stories but favourite voices. The best have a quality of song, of incantation.

All of the stories in this collection induced me at one moment or another to hold my breath. They have been well chosen, not just in their variety but in their capacity to weave a spell. What is novel here is that each story is accompanied by an essay in which the writer speaks about her or his inspiration and method. All good stories, no matter how spontaneous and artless they appear on the surface, are the products of an acute organising intelligence, one that makes dozens and even hundreds of decisions in the course of writing several drafts. The workings of this intelligence are laid out for us in the essays. We are offered insights into the wrought quality of the process, a mixture of dream-like speculation and hammer and anvil constructedness. We observe the humility that good writers bring to their material, the care with which they approach it, their disdain for the trite or the obvious, the degree to which they feel called to do justice. Justice is a big thing for writers, an aspect of their motivation, and their art, not often enough discussed. These essays make us more fully aware of how that desire for justice informs a story and the reasons why and ways in which writers make of their ethical preoccupations not a treatise but a narrative.

But the stories in this collection need no explication; they stand alone as accomplished works. Rather is it the case that the essays are stories in another form. They are a rare bonus.

—Amanda Lohrey, 2014

EDITORS' NOTE

Where did the idea for *Cracking the Spine* come from? As authors and as teachers of the short story, we are both fascinated by the genre and by the writing practice of others. There are, however, few opportunities to read the stories behind the stories.

Spineless Wonders regularly posts interviews with Australian writers on its blog, *The Column*. Overwhelmingly, it is the responses which explore process that readers and writers find most engaging. So the idea of collating this material in book form, of making it more accessible, was born.

In *Cracking the Spine* we moved away from the interview format to the essay – to allow a more in-depth exploration not only of a specific story but of the author's preoccupations and concerns.

This collection is not exhaustive. We have selected these ten authors for the range of style, subject matter and themes their stories and essays explored. We could have selected many others, and hope to do so in future publications.

We hope *Cracking the Spine* will be a valuable and inspiring resource for senior high school and university teachers and their students as well as general readers.

Thanks to the Literature Board of the Australia Council for funding this project. And thanks to the contributors for the creativity, openness and generosity with which they responded to our requests.

—Julie Chevalier *and* Bronwyn Mehan

CRACKING THE SPINE

Ten short Australian stories
and how they were written

PETER CAREY Collected Stories
Australian Love Stories
GILES
•FROM THE VERANDAH•
helen GARNER
a COCK HORSE
Gillian MEARS
The PENGUIN CENTURY of AUSTRALIAN STORIES
EDITED BY CARMEL BIRD
VIKING
MS
ESCAPE
SHORT AUSTRALIAN STORIES
SMALL INDISCRETIONS
EMMETT STINSON
The Rattler & other stories
A. S. Patrić
Dark Roots
Cate Kennedy

'AN AUSTRALIAN SHORT STORY'

Ryan O'Neill

It is a Tuesday morning.[1]

It was a plain weatherboard house, with a rose garden at the front, a vegetable garden down the side, and an orchard at the back.[2] Everything about the place groaned with bad taste.[3] Its solidity was late nineteenth century, as the town's was.[4] Two parrots perched on the white and blue fence, preening themselves from their fluffy orange chests to their green tails, their wings opening and closing, their necks twisting and turning.[5] The landscape of red tin roofs shimmered liquid in the heat.[6] All over the district the smell of smoke, charred wood and incinerated gum leaves tinged the air and thickened with every breeze.[7]

Then, to the right, at the far end of the house, a jacaranda tree in shadow seemed to disintegrate and its pieces scatter as a flock of birds rose from its branches.[8] For a moment he stood uncertainly in the sun, then ran back into the she-oaks.[9] He was a short, thickset man of about forty-two years of age; his face was not handsome by any means, but the features and the expression of his face was something very peculiar.[10] His breathing was tired and heavy, sometimes catching and whistling softly in some mysterious passage behind his chest.[11]

Shit, he thought, his life was a mess.[12] He achieved, tangibly, nothing on his farm, if such it could be called.[13] As usual he attracted women who wished to still the raging storms of his heart.[14] But there was, to all appearance, but small hope of that.[15] Worst of all, the unaskable question – was he happy with her?[16]

She might have materialised piecemeal in his mind, her black hair drawn smooth and tight to be held at her neck, the whiteness of the scalp where the strong hair was pulled back from her forehead, her full arms and the slope of her almost bare shoulders, her skin as if not much exposed to the sun and with its own flush of colour – these things came to him like unrelated aspects of different people.[17]

'Hullo,' she said, standing flat-footed in her cheap thongs, the breeze pressing the thin folds of the long green dress against the backs of her thighs.[18] 'I thought you had a story you wanted to finish.'[19]

'No, no, it's all right.'[20] He grinned as if he had found his true love, and perhaps he had.[21]

He said he must have some smell which repels publishers.[22]

'I don't think so,' she murmured, and smiled, although the smile was also something of a murmur.[23]

'Happiness,' he said, 'is notoriously difficult to describe.'[24]

Her husband's gaze caught hers; he waited, challenging.[25]

'Yes,' she said.[26]

'I've been writing a novel,' he added.[27]

Suddenly she felt like crying.[28] Her mind was still numb from the cold winter and what she saw as the gradual failure of her marriage.[29]

His eyes clouded over in revulsion.[30] 'You don't even care.'[31]

A couple of pages, that was all, in two years.[32]

'I'm sorry...'[33] She assumed a bleak, set expression, trying to ward off the idiotic butterfly smile that persisted in trying to alight on her mouth.[34]

'Curse you!' he yelled.[35]

It had come over him again, for no reason – the feeling of failure, of isolation that this landscape had given him.[36]

'You're always saying that, for years you've said it.'[37] He stopped suddenly and stared in front of him.[38] What the landscape had to say to him under these circumstances was not precisely clear.[39]

She began to grumble her way across the yard and into the house.[40] 'One thing I do know,' she was trembling with rage, 'the one thing I'm sure of is that I've been too good to you.'[41]

'Go away.[42] I feel like I'm suffocating.'[43]

She gazed at him with a puzzled frown as if trying to divine exactly what he meant.[44]

'Say that again and you will put me into a passion.'[45]

'I'm sick of you.'[46] (He didn't remember saying any of this, later on.)[47]

'It's only this,' she said suddenly, 'I can't stand this life here; it will kill me!'[48]

A roar of laughter was the reply.[49]

She was walking away; she was no longer between him and the light.[50]

'Dirty brute!' she said.[51] 'I won't be returning.[52] Goodbye.'[53]

Distance seemed to have a soporific effect on him.[54]

'Goodbye,' he called, and it was as if a tree had spoken.[55]

*

In the weeks after his wife left, each crowd was a riot, each street a midnight alley.[56] He would dawdle down to the harbour, with its green smell of sea lettuce and the stone wall, scribbled with the white droppings of gulls.[57] The air was full of gulls and the stench of sheep ships and harbour scum.[58] He blundered past a man sharpening his fingernails on a red brick wall, a bare-faced waitress swabbing terrace tables, a busker unpacking a saxophone in a doorway.[59] He took off his hat, dropped it carelessly on the ground, and proceeded to business.[60]

The pub.[61] That's when he started to drink.[62]

The vintners fetched wine fit to make you drunk, smooth on the tongue and rufous, rough as a dog's rasp at some abdominal cavity which finds gentility a bore, but fairly clear of histamines, thank Christ.[63] Of course, his wife never understood him, that was the trouble, such a queer, difficult kind of woman.[64] He looked up at the sky.[65] A hundred yards out, just beyond the line of surf, two seagulls were hovering.[66] It was all part of the quivering awareness of the natural world.[67] He felt confused and helpless.[68] 'What am I supposed to do?' he said.[69] Let me, for God's sweet sake, get drunk.[70]

He was red-eyed, bleared and unsteady.[71] So many, many fights.[72] All the time she'd worked and gone without and lived in the heat and believed in them, and close to the time he could make those things up to her she should go.[73] More fine wines are produced, more savouring of the crystal goblets.[74] His lips moved as if he were addressing some image held before his inner vision; then he turned and tramped on.[75] How could it have turned into such a fucking disaster?[76]

'Jesus Christ!' he said, covering his eyes.[77]

The sun was getting low now, and the shadows were lengthening.[78]

*

It was evening, after a day hot enough to blister the ear of an elephant.[79] When he got to the house the front was dark, but he could see light coming from the kitchen at the back.[80] The miracle had happened.[81] A voice boomed out of the blackness.[82]

'If you have anything to say to me, sir,' (the dusky pale of her cheeks illuminated by two spots of crimson) 'you had better say it.'[83]

He stood very still with his face lifted towards the house, as a tradesmen waits who has rung the doorbell, received no answer, and hopes that someone will appear at last at an upper window.[84]

'I'd like to explain.'[85]

'What?'[86]

'Why are you weeping?'[87]

A sorrow beyond words.[88]

'Oh, nothing,' she paused.[89] '...anyone could, we could all cry like that every day if we wanted to, if we didn't stop ourselves.'[90]

The weight of her dress was lifted outwards and the moon was in her face.[91]

'You'll admit,' said her husband, 'that you tend to the dramatic.[92]

She laughed at this to herself.[93]

So he began to feel a good deal better.[94]

'My love for you,' he said, 'is the most honourable thing about me.'[95]

She smiled her sideways smile.[96]

'Love's fucked, anyway.'[97]

She caught his arm and walked him through the front door, and down the carpeted hall to their bedroom.[98] They were entering Paradise.[99] On occasions like this, his face was a mask of glee, grinning with self-satisfaction, as though he'd pulled off a particularly difficult conjuring trick.[100] He put his hand on her knee and rested it there.[101] Does she love him?[102] She rests her hands on his shoulders; he puts his arms around her.[103] The clasp seemed to embolden her to confidence.[104] A dance, fleshed out by smouldering fantasies, a heartbeat of time so intense it is unbearable, wallowing in velvet so soft you can feel each hair brushing like silk against your skin.[105] And he presses his crying mouth into her flesh.[106]

At last he fell back exhausted, and lay breathing heavily.[107] 'Are you happy now then?'[108]

Thanks, that was nice, she said.[109] But her heart was beating pit-a-pat.[110]

'Just trying to keep things together,' he muttered before he nodded off.[111]

His breathing, a solid snore of the same pitch and volume hour after hour, night after night, was as comforting as the sea.[112] He was woken in the night by a dream of intercourse, the excitement of fondling a body, the huge relief of orgasm.[113] He raised himself upon his elbow noiselessly and peered into the darkness.[114] He stood up and walked out of the room.[115] He sat in the lounge in the vague – the vain – hope that she might actually follow him.[116] A universal dictionary, a rhyming dictionary, a thesaurus, an illustrated bestiary, inks of various colours and consistencies, pencils of all hardnesses, penhandles of many shapes, and pens of steel, quill and gold, were all fitted into a combination lectern and writing desk, which held also a dictaphone, an improved pantograph for writing by hand, and a stenotype machine.[117] He suddenly loved the place at night, its stillness, its lights, its easy beauty.[118] He lifted the peg-board from beside his chair, adjusted the wad of unruled paper, and began to write generously across it with a blue felt pen.[119] Scenes, conversations, faces.[120] The man buried himself in his paper.[121]

The night wore on.[122] Towards dawn, his eyes heavy and his mind exhausted, he would catch himself nodding in his chair, and would return to bed.[123]

'How is your writing?' she asked.[124]

'Vanity,' he cried, 'all is vanity.'[125]

'I'm sure your novel, when you get down to it, will be excellent.'[126]

This became her answer to everything.[127]

'What is sad,' he said, 'is that I've learned some of these things more than once.'[128]

'Do you have a theory about everything,' she asked tiredly.[129]

What he felt he kept within his breast.[130] He could not help being a little selfish; it was constitutional.[131] She has seen it year after year after year.[132] Indeed, she was as proud of it as of his talent, of which she considered it an expression.[133]

'Do you love me?'[134]

'Of course,' she whispered back and sinking down reached up both arms to him.[135]

His eyes danced a little, and she noticed in them a life hitherto kept from her sight.[136] Was she, with the smile no anguish could unpin, and no agony subdue, happy?[137] She must make do with what is available to be offered.[138]

'You're sure?'[139]

'Yes![140] You believe me?'[141]

'Yes.'[142]

And she lay beside him, separated by a knowledge which he did not share, of something sinister; of wounding, of unhappiness and of pain.[143]

She laughed.[144] 'Very well, I'll tell you a story.'[145]

They would live – somewhere, and be – very happy.[146] Tomorrow will be full of possibilities.[147] She lied and lied and lied.[148]

And she hugs him to her worn-out breast and kisses him; and they sit thus together while the sickly daylight breaks over the bush.[149]

Endnotes

1 'Reconstruction of an Event' by Glenda Adams (1979)
2 'American Dreams' by Peter Carey (1974)
3 'Hunting the Wild Pineapple' by Thea Astley (1979)
4 'Gretel' by Hal Porter (1963)
5 'A Fishbone in the Throat' by Isabelle Li (2009)
6 'Salt' by Pierz Newton-John (2009)
7 'The Funerals' by Brian Matthews (1989)
8 'Little Jackie' by A.G. McNeil (2009)
9 'Under the House' by Jessica Anderson (1980)
10 'The Master and his Man' by John Lang (1859)
11 'Dust' by Gavin Casey (1936)
12 'Sonatina' by Brian Castro (1994)
13 'The Man of Callemondah' by David Rowbotham (1956)
14 'The Last Days of a Famous Mime' by Peter Carey (1974)
15 'A Dispersal' by Anon (c 1850)
16 'The Powerful Owl' by Candida Baker (1994)
17 'Party' by Peter Cowan (1965)
18 'Nails of Love, Nails of Death' by James McQueen (1984)
19 'A Man in the Laundrette' by Beverley Farmer (1985)
20 'Place of Birth' by Beverley Farmer (1985)
21 'The Punch' by Laurie Steed (2010)
22 'New York, New York' by Rosemary Creswell (1986)
23 'The Booster Shot' by Peter Goldsworthy (1993)
24 'Portrait of Electricity' by Murray Bail (1975)
25 'The List of All Answers' by Peter Goldsworthy (1986)
26 'The Milk' by Jessica Anderson (1987)
27 'The Other Side of the River' by Georgia Blain (2009)
28 'A,B,C,D,E,F,G,H,I,J,K,L,M,N,O,P,Q,R,S,T,U,V,W,X,Y,Z' by Murray Bail (1975)
29 'Country Girl Again' by Jean Bedford (1979)
30 'Going Home' by Archie Weller (1986)
31 'Nullarbor Honeymoon' by Dorothy Hewitt (1996)
32 'Our Lady of the Beehives' by Beverley Farmer (1985)
33 'The Shipwreck Party' by Liam Davison (1989)
34 'The Weight of a Man' by Amy Witting (1961)
35 'How Muster-Master Stoneman Earned his Breakfast' by Price Warung (real name William Astley) (1892)

36 'The Weeping Fig' by Judith Wright (1953)
37 'Frederick the Great Returns to Fairfields' by Elizabeth Jolley (1983)
38 'Miss Jackson' by Francis Adams (1892)
39 'An Old-Time Episode in Tasmania' by Tasma (real name Jessie Couvreur) (1891)
40 'Down at the Dump' by Patrick White (1964)
41 'Hostages' by Fay Zwicky (1983)
42 'What Else is There?' by Margaret Trist (1946)
43 'Las Vegas for Vegans' by A.S. Patrić (2011)
44 'Well, What Do You Say to My Boy?' by Judah L. Waten (1954)
45 'The Ghost upon the Rail' by John Lang (1859)
46 'Fiend and Friend' by Hal Porter (1962)
47 'New Year' by Joan London (1986)
48 'Water Them Geraniums' by Henry Lawson (1904)
49 'The Parson's Blackboy' by Ernest Favenc (1893)
50 'The Only Adam' by Gerald Murnane (1985)
51 'Uncle Patrick was a Scholar' by Margaret Trist (1946)
52 'Period Piece on the 'Fields' by Lyndall Hadow (1962)
53 'Oh I Do Love to be Beside the Seaside' by J.M.S. Foster (1980)
54 'The Sleeping Doll' by John Morrison (1955)
55 'Trees Can Speak' by Alan Marshall (1956)
56 'Flinch' by Ryan O'Neill (2007)
57 'Clay' by Patrick White (1964)
58 'Thomas Awkner Floats' by Tim Winton (1985)
59 'A Vigil' by Helen Garner (1992)
60 'The Union Buries its Dead' by Henry Lawson (1892)
61 'Short-Shift Saturday' by Gavin Casey (1942)
62 'Miracle of the Waters' by Zeny Giles (1989)
63 'I Lost my Love to the Space Shuttle *Columbia*' by Damien Broderick (1986)
64 'The Letter' by Marjorie Robertson (1946)
65 'Velodrome' by Angelo Loukakis (1986)
66 'The Birthday' by Vance Palmer (1934)
67 'The Dingo' by Vance Palmer (1934)
68 'The Woman from the Bend' by Don Edwards (1944)

69 'Solemn Mass' by Dal Stivens (1941)
70 'A Double Because It's Snowing' by Hal Porter (1958)
71 'Hawkins' Pigs' by Brian James (1944)
72 'I Told Mama Not to Come' by Angelo Loukakis (1983)
73 'Living' by Peter Cowan (1944)
74 'I Am Monarch of All I Survey' by Michael Wilding (1986)
75 'The Good Herdsman' by Frank Dalby Davison (1964)
76 'Partying on Parquet' by Angelo Loukakis (1986)
77 'The Chosen Vessel' by Barbara Baynton (1902)
78 'The Brown Paper Coffin' by James McQueen (1988)
79 'Mr and Mrs Sin Fat' by Edward Dyson (1890)
80 'Did He Pay?' by Helen Garner (1981)
81 'The Miracle' by A.E. Sturges (1963)
82 'Reunion in Gunyah Creek' by Maurice Corlett (1980)
83 'The Romance of Lively Creek' by Marcus Clarke (1877)
84 'The Empty Lunch-Tin' by David Malouf (1985)
85 'Graffito Spy' by C.C. Catt (1981)
86 'Having a Wonderful Time' by Kate Grenville (1980)
87 'Life and Death in the South Side Pavilion' by Peter Carey (1975)
88 'The Lost World: Signs of Life' by Ted Colless and David Kelly (1983)
89 'Extra Virgin' by Jan Hutchinson (1988)
90 'Working Hot' by Mary Fallon (1982)
91 'The Incomparable' by Nicholas Jose (1984)
92 'The Enemies of Time' by Amy Witting (1991)
93 'From a Bush Log Book: Going into the Heartlands with the Wrong Person at Christmas' by Frank Moorhouse (1981)
94 'The Narrow Escape of Herbie Bassett' by Eleanor Dark (1959)
95 'The Heraldry of the Body' by Craig McGregor (1983)
96 'The Midnight Supper' by David Campbell (1959)
97 'Campaign' by Jean Bedford (1985)
98 'The Cost of Things' by Elizabeth Harrower (1974)
99 'Paradise' by Murray Bail (1975)
100 'Waiting for Mr Mowbray' by Paul Morgan (2008)
101 'The Art of Convalescence' by Amanda Lohrey (2009)
102 'The Courts of the Lord' by Fay Zwicky (1983)

103 'Foxtrot' by Claire Aman (2009)
104 'Miss Pallavant' by Rosa Praed (1888)
105 'Queen of Love' by Rosie Scott (1989)
106 'An Unfinished Head' by Carolyn Van Langenberg (1986)
107 'The Premier's Secret' by Campbell McKellar (1887)
108 'The Bodies' by Michael Sala (2009)
109 'Our Swimmer' by Tim Richards (1992)
110 'And Women Must Weep' by Henry Handel Richardson (1934)
111 'Breaking Up' by Paddy O'Reilly (2008)
112 'Mermaid Footwear' by G.L. Osborne (2009)
113 'The Man of Slow Feeling' by Michael Wilding (1970)
114 'The Heart-Breaking of Anstey's Bess' by Price Warung (real name William Astley) (1894)
115 'Amateur Hour' by Garry Disher (1986)
116 'Getting to the Pig' by Barry Hill (1978)
117 'Guest of the Redshields' by Christina Stead (1934)
118 'The Sybarites' by Michael Wilding (1972)
119 'Virgins, Widows and Penitents' by Gerard Windsor (1980)
120 'Angel' by Cate Kennedy (2006)
121 'Lady Weare and the Bodhisattva' by Kylie Tennant (1969)
122 'The Night We Watched for Wallabies' by Steele Rudd (1899)
123 'Dr B. and the Students' by David Brooks (1990)
124 'Conrad's Bear' by Susan Hampton (1984)
125 'A Knight of Teeth' by Peter Mathers (1981)
126 'An Extraordinary Thing' by Ray Mathew (1961)
127 'How I Met my Daughter' by Max Barry (2007)
128 'Libido and Life Lessons' by Frank Moorhouse (1987)
129 'The Airport, the Pizzeria, the Motel, the Rented Car and the Mysteries of Life' by Frank Moorhouse (1977)
130 'The Story of Wills' Leap' by R. Spencer Browne (1890)
131 'The Luckiest Man in the Colony' by E.W. Hornung (1892)
132 'The Crossing' by Deborah Robertson (1992)
133 'Kaijek the Songman' by Xavier Herbert (1941)
134 'Do You Love Me?' by Peter Carey (1979)
135 'The Rages of Mrs Torrens' by Olga Masters (1982)
136 'The Swallows Returning' by Ian Kennedy Williams (1982)
137 'Young Woman in a Wimple' by Hal Porter (1963)

138 'Reasons for Going into Gynaecology' by Gerard Windsor (1984)
139 'Ismini' by Beverley Farmer (1983)
140 'The Price' by H. Drake-Brockman (1941)
141 'Green Grow the Rushes' by T.A.G. Hungerford (1976)
142 'Running Nicely' by Morris Lurie (1979)
143 'Winter Nelis' by Elizabeth Jolley (1979)
144 'Mauve' by Patrick Cullen (2009)
145 'Sojur Jim' by J.A. Barry (1893)
146 'The Cost of Things' by Elizabeth Harrower (1967)
147 'Summer in Sydney' by Barbara Brooks (1983)
148 'Boy Meets Girl' by Hal Porter (1980)
149 'The Drover's Wife' by Henry Lawson (1892)

HOW TO READ AN AUSTRALIAN SHORT STORY

essay by Ryan O'Neill

Before I came to Australia in 2004, I had never read an Australian short story. I had never heard of Henry Lawson, despite Frank Hardy's hyperbolic claim that Lawson 'in the short stories written between 1889 and 1895, was beyond question the greatest short story writer in the world, surpassing Chekhov and de Maupassant'.[1] I had never even read any Patrick White, though I suspect this is something I have in common with most Australians. In fact, I had only ever read two Australian novels: *For the Term of his Natural Life* by Marcus Clarke, and *Illywhacker* by Peter Carey. I enjoyed both of these books, but thought at the time that they were just too long. Years later, I would discover the short fiction of Clarke and Carey, and they would become two of my favourite short story writers.

I think my ignorance of the Australian short story was pardonable, considering I was born and brought up in Scotland, and attended a university in Glasgow that didn't offer any courses on the short story, Scottish, Australian or otherwise. It wasn't until soon after arriving in Australia, then, that I read my first Australian short fiction. Browsing in a secondhand bookshop, I picked up a copy of *The Penguin Century of Australian Stories*,[2] edited by Carmel Bird. This proved to be an inspired choice, as the anthology is an excellent introduction to the Australian short story, despite the rather odd decision to list the stories alphabetically by author, rather than chronologically by publication.

I hadn't known quite what to expect from Australian short fiction, so I was delighted to see that among the many stories that could be termed 'realist' – dealing as they did with ordinary people, and everyday events, and told in a straightforward style without formal or stylistic experimentation – there were quite a few stories that departed from the norm, such as 'The Man of Slow Feeling' by Michael Wilding, or 'A Snake Down Under' by Glenda Adams. Although I had written my own share of traditional, realist fiction, at that time I was becoming more and more interested in telling stories in less traditional ways, such as in the broken English of a Lithuanian schoolgirl, or in a story told in six different tenses.

However, it wasn't long before I realised that while *The Penguin Century of Australian Stories* was an outstanding anthology, it was not entirely a representative one. The majority of the selected stories were from the 1980s and 1990s, obscuring the fact that most Australian short fiction, past and present, did not greatly experiment in style, theme or form. In truth, the Australian short story tradition was generally one of realism in style and content. The most influential of all Australian short story writers appeared a diffident sixty-first in *The Penguin Century of Australian Stories.* I remember reading 'The Loaded Dog' and not thinking much of it, preferring the Joan London piece that followed it. The writer of 'The Loaded Dog' was Henry Lawson.

The impact of Henry Lawson on the Australian short story can't be overstated. Before Lawson, there were, of course, Australian short story writers, such as Mary Fortune, or 'Tasma', very talented though little read today. These writers would skilfully utilise the setting of the Australian bush, but would often people it with stock characters from English novels. Alternatively, they could create convincing Australian characters, but forced them with varying degrees of success into pre-existing literary templates such as the Gothic or Detective story, imported from Britain and America. If

Henry Lawson was not the first to successfully marry a uniquely Australian style and content (Marcus Clarke had done this before him), he was certainly the most successful. Lawson's stories were told in an unpretentious, unadorned prose style that was, in some ways, astonishingly modern. Lawson's minimalist style anticipated that of the more celebrated Ernest Hemingway by thirty years, as can be seen in the following two extracts, the first from a Lawson story, the second from a Hemingway.

> He turned away to put up the rails. The lower rail went into its place all right, but the top one had got jammed, and it stuck as though it was spiked. He worked the rail up and down and to and fro, took it under his arm and tugged it; but he might as well have pulled at one of the posts. Then he lifted the loose end as high as he could and let it fall – jumping back out of the way at the same time; this loosened it, but when he lifted it again it slid so easily and far into its socket that the other end came out, and fell, barking Brook's knee. He swore a little, then tackled the rail again; he had the same trouble as before with the other end, but succeeded at last. Then he turned away, rubbing his knee.
>
> Lizzie hadn't smiled, not once; she watched him gravely all the while.
>
> 'Did you hurt your knee?' she asked without emotion.
>
> 'No. The rail did.'
>
> She reflected solemnly for a while, and then asked him if it felt sore.
>
> He replied rather briefly in the negative.
>
> 'They were always nasty, awkward rails to put up,' she remarked, after some more reflection.
>
> Brook agreed, and then they turned their faces towards the homestead.
>
> ('An Unfinished Love Story' by Henry Lawson)

> She came in with the boat and ran the second line out the same way. Each time Nick set a heavy slab of driftwood across the butt of the road to hold it solid and propped it up at an angle with a small slab. He reeled in the slack line so the line ran taut out to where the bait rested on the sandy floor of the channel and set the click on the reel. When a trout, feeding on the bottom, took the bait it would run with it, taking line out of the reel in a rush and making the reel sing with the click on.
>
> Marjorie rowed up to the point a little way so she would not disturb the line. She pulled hard on the oars and the boat went up the beach. Little waves came with it. Marjorie stepped out of the boat and Nick pulled the boat high up on the beach.
>
> 'What's the matter, Nick?' Marjorie asked.
>
> 'I don't know,' Nick said, getting wood for a fire.
>
> They made a fire with driftwood.
>
> ('The End of Something' by Ernest Hemingway)

If the names of the authors were removed from these extracts, I would challenge any reader to decide which had been written in Australia in the 1890s, and which in America in the 1920s.

Lawson's stories had little in common with the melodramatic ciphers that featured in other Australian short fiction of the time. His characters were not lords or pirates, or convicts, but farmers and their wives, swagmen and drovers, and they existed in a recognisably and uniquely Australian landscape, and spoke in an authentic Australian dialect. Lawson's success and influence were not only due to his skill as a writer, but also owed something to when he was published. His stories, written at the turn of the twentieth century, were seized upon and celebrated by an Australian press and public eager to cement their newly federated nation's individuality. Lawson provided a view of Australia that Australians found attractive, in a style that Australians found readable. For Michael Wilding this resulted in 'a nationalist cult of the short story, with Henry Lawson as the particular native genius and fount and source. The Australian story began with Lawson, the myth read: so anthology after anthology of Australian short stories was produced beginning with Lawson'.[3] Wilding could perhaps be accused of overstating the case against Lawson, but it is true that many Australian short story anthologies ignore writers active in the form before him, and in their selection favour stories written in a Lawsonian vein – that is, in a realist mode, and in a straightforward style.

The impact and uniqueness of Lawson's short stories have been blunted by his many imitators. It can therefore be easy to forget that Lawson's stories were, for their time, experimental; he was writing about subjects few had written about before in a way few had done before. His best stories, such as 'The Drover's Wife' and 'The Union Buries its Dead', were instantly acclaimed, and recognised as something new in Australian fiction, and it didn't take long before other writers followed the path Lawson had blazed, beginning 'The Lawson Tradition' in the Australian short story. Foremost among Lawson's contemporaries was Steele Rudd, whose seemingly endless series of *On Our Selection* short stories appropriated Lawson's commonplace themes, unpretentious style and bush setting, but replaced his skill and pathos with evermore wearying slapstick and sentimentality. Other, and better, writers followed Lawson, almost always working skilfully within the parameters he had set, but seldom challenging them. There were many great Australian short stories written in the first half of the twentieth century, but to even the most attentive reader they tend, if read one after another, to blend into one long story told in a determinedly realist style, with a bush setting, working-class characters, and a screen door eternally banging in the wind. The short stories selected for the 1967 anthology *Short Stories of Australia: The Lawson Tradition*[4], demonstrated the enduring, and sometimes suffocating, influence of Lawson's style and subject matter, at least through to the 1940s. For the editors of this anthology, the Australian short story, quite simply, began with Henry Lawson.

Though Patrick White was perhaps cruel in describing this style of writing as 'the dreary, dun-coloured offspring of journalistic realism', it can't be denied that there is a certain feeling of 'brownness' to a lot of Australian short fiction up until the 1970s. Lawson had staked out an original territory, but his followers over farmed and exhausted it. By the 1920s and 1930s, the modernist movement in the USA and Europe had abandoned many of the literary conventions that Australian fiction was to cling to for far too long. Whereas realist writers saw reality as something that existed independent of the observer, modernist writers saw it as existing only so far as it was experienced and refracted through individual consciousness. Thus, in the great modernist novels such as *The Sound and the Fury*, *Parade's End* and *To the Lighthouse* plot and time were no longer linear, as reality was distorted through the eyes of the characters. Yet in this era of great literary experimentation, the Australian short story, with a few exceptions (such as 'The Persimmon Tree' by Marjorie Barnard, and the tall tales of Dal Stivens), continued in Lawson's dryly realist style, following laconic characters who lived in the bush, and a plot that plodded from beginning to middle to end, almost always in that order. It could be argued that modernism did not finally arrive in Australia until the novels and stories of Patrick White, and it had barely settled down before postmodernism followed in the 1970s.

Postmodernism, rather than modifying realist conventions, abandoned them. The idea of any kind of 'reality' was called into question, as was traditional fiction's ability to represent it in any meaningful way. Self-reflexivity came to the fore; no longer were writers to conceal themselves from the reader, but instead they became part of the story, commenting on and criticising it. In Australian terms the 1970s saw a revolution in subject matter and form. Out was the bush, in was the city. Out was the screen door, in was the hash pipe. Out was 'D-mn!' and in was 'Fuck!' Out were realist stories, in were stories told through chain letters, fantasies, a hundred different forms. Short story writers such as Michael Wilding, Frank Moorhouse and Vicki Viidikas broached topics that would have been taboo only a few years before. This new freedom in exploring different themes was mirrored in the exploration of genres and forms long neglected or sidelined in Australia, including science fiction and the surreal. In this decade, Moorhouse, Peter Carey and Murray Bail produced a number of brilliant short stories, perhaps the best ever produced in this country. Though the Australian short story would return to its realist roots in the 1980s and beyond, it would never be as 'brown' again.

While Australian short fiction was dominated by men for much of the 1970s, the latter part of that decade as well as the one that followed saw a flowering of brilliant realist and experimental stories written by women. From the misfits populating Thea Astley's north Queensland in 'Hunting the Wild Pineapple' to the stories of liars and writers in Glenda Adams' 'The Hottest Night of the Century' and the rehabilitation of a more modern realism in the stories of Elizabeth Jolley and Helen Garner, the 1980s remained an exciting time for Australian short fiction. Throughout the 1990s and the twenty-first century, realism came to reassert itself as the predominant literary mode of Australian short fiction, but though the experimental was never to again attain the dominance it enjoyed in the 1970s, it maintained a steady presence in the work of writers such as David Brooks, A.S. Patrić, Ania Walwicz, Tom Cho and others.

All of which brings us, in a very roundabout way, to 'An Australian Short Story'. I can't quite remember when I had the idea for this piece, but I know it was in the middle of an Australian short fiction reading binge. I had just finished several anthologies published in the 1940s and 1950s, and then, without knowing quite what was coming, leapt into one of the great, formally daring collections of the 1970s, Murray Bail's *Contemporary Portraits and Other Stories.*[5] In my imagination, the traditional themes and style of the earlier stories collided with Bail's playfulness, and I wondered if it would be possible to write a short story entirely made up of lines from other Australian short stories. Writing under constraints was something that had interested me for a long time. I had read and enjoyed several of the books that had emerged from the French Oulipo movement, which encouraged writers to take risks in style and form. Georges Perec's *A Void*, for example, is a novel written without using the letter e. The Oulipians believed that writing under a constraint would actually free up a writer's creativity, and this proved to be the case in writing 'An Australian Short Story'.

First, I visited the university library, and borrowed all the Australian short story collections and anthologies I could find. Added to my own books, including my old favourite *The Penguin Century of Australian Stories*, I had a bank of perhaps a thousand short stories to choose from. One additional constraint I set myself was that I could only use one line from one particular story, though there was nothing to stop me using multiple stories from the same writer. (When reading 'An Australian Short Story' again recently for this anthology, I noticed that I had inadvertently broken this constraint by having two lines from the same story by Elizabeth Harrower. I've decided to let them stand, as I love those lines, and after all, rules are meant to be broken.) There were no restrictions on when the stories were written, only that the authors were Australian. I spent several evenings going through these stories with a notepad by my side, noting down lines that struck me for any reason. I soon came to realise that the constraints I was writing under posed a number of unique problems, the first of which was the plot. Usually, before I begin writing, I have to know the broad outlines of the plot, and preferably the first and last line of the story. But coming up with a plot, and finding lines to flesh it out proved to be impossible. Instead, the plot would have to write itself. Also, the number of characters in the story would have to be limited, and the characters could not have names, as it was unlikely I would find enough stories that included, for example, a character called 'John'.

Soon I had perhaps thirty or forty lines, which I then clustered together under different headings such as 'Setting', 'Description of him', 'Description of her', 'Movement', and so on. I then trawled through more stories, noting down additional lines that might be used. This proved to be a laborious process, as I not only had to keep track of the line, but the story it came from, and who wrote it. Finally, the selection process was finished, and I had found a few hundred promising sentences that I thought I could use. By then I had some idea of the plot; it would be a love story. Now I knew what I wanted to happen in the story, I dreaded 'writing' it. I thought the reassembling of the lines into a coherent whole would be a nightmare, but it proved to be the easiest part of the process. Within only a couple of hours, whether through luck or good judgement, each of the sentences slotted neatly into place to create a story, of sorts.

There were gaps, of course, sections that required an action or a line of dialogue that I hadn't yet found. In these cases I returned to the anthologies and collections, and combed the pages looking for a particular movement or description that would fit in the blank space of my story. This could have been frustrating, but instead it was strangely addictive, like putting together the final pieces of a jigsaw. At last, I only had one essential line that I was unable to find – I needed something to show that the woman had left the man. It was the turning point of the story. I hadn't intended in using any lines from my own work in 'An Australian Short Story', but finally I grew sick of searching for the perfect line, and settled for a suitable one from my story 'Flinch'. The first and last lines of 'An Australian Short Story' were the last to be 'written', the opposite of how I usually work. I wanted to begin the story with a writer who was not afraid to experiment with form, and so I chose Glenda Adams, and I wanted to end with the most influential Australian short story writer of all, Henry Lawson, and the most famous line from his most famous story.

I had originally intended for this piece to be a satire. 'An Australian Short Story' was titled 'The Australian Short Story' for a long time, to suggest the idea that, with its bush setting, and sentimental love story, it was somehow representative of a certain uniformity in Australian short fiction. But as I finished the story I was surprised and pleased to see it had developed into more of a celebration than a satire. I can say without boasting that 'An Australian Short Story' is beautifully written, with memorable imagery and some marvellous lines of dialogue. I like to think that this story proves the Australian short story tradition is not as dreary and dun coloured as White maintained; rather, if examined just a little more closely, it becomes a glorious patchwork.

Endnotes

1. Frank Hardy quote from *Australian Literary Studies*, vol. 10.2, October 1981, 'The Contemporary Australian Short Story Special Issue', p202.

2. Bird, C. (ed.) 2000, *The Penguin Century of Australian Stories*, Penguin Australia, Ringwood, Victoria.

3. Wilding, M. (ed.) 1978, *The Tabloid Story Pocket Book,* Wild & Woolley, 1978, Sydney, p303.

4. Stewart, D. (ed.) 1967, *Short Stories of Australia: The Lawson Tradition*, Angus and Robertson, Sydney.

5. Bail, M. 1975, *Contemporary Portraits and other stories*, University of Queensland Press, St. Lucia, Qld.

АНТОНЪ ЧЕХОВЪ.

ТРИ СЕСТРЫ

ДРАМА

въ 4-хъ дѣйствіяхъ.

ИЗДАНІЕ

А.Ф. МАРКСА.

С.ПЕТЕРБУРГЪ.

'THREE SISTERS'

Maria Takolander

Let us take a look at this place. Marshlands. All the way to the horizon. The land drained, but nevertheless sinking. Sinking into nothing, nothing but itself. Frogs volleying noise in the grass, unseen. The hazy movement of mosquitoes low to the ground. On a lush blade of green a sleek cricket, blacker than night and – look closely – its antennae twitching. Just think: there must be more of those creatures, thousands, perhaps millions, clinging to the swamp grass as far as your eye can see.

Running through it all is the highway: black tarmac dumped on a man-made ridge. Power poles no longer vertical. Wires sagging. And a tarmac bridge, built without so much as a timber railing. Can you see the creek underneath? A seam of brown water between banks of mud. The mud pockmarked with crab holes and mangrove-ridden.

There is firmer land somewhere. Land where cattle stamp the soil with cloven hooves. Where horse hair is torn against barbed fences. Where colossal windmills slice the air. But that is not here.

Now, the terror of a road train – listen! Tearing at the asphalt, shaking its steel hinges, like a caged animal, angry only at itself. See how it passes in a tumult of wind. Even the murky water of the creek shudders. Then the swamp grass settles. The frogs resume their hollow sound-making. The cricket has gone.

Look around in the stillness abandoned by the truck's passing. There is a cluster of weatherboard houses. Crouched past the bridge, in the clearing by the muddy creek. See the white one-room bungalow? With the peeling paint and the skeletons of fish hanging from the porch like a witchdoctor's bunting? That is a museum.

On the walls inside you will find a collection of colourless photographs. Aerial surveys. A fishing boat in a vein of water, closed in by mangroves. A group of moustachioed men, holding onto the rails of a wooden jetty. Eyeing the camera as if it was an enemy. There is a creature from prehistory, all tendrils and feathery gills, hauled up on a chain next to them. And look: another picture. On the muddy bank, a sorry group of men, almost naked, forlorn as the forgotten.

So much for the museum. Do you see, on the other side of the highway, the white clapboard building? It is the roadhouse. The only one for miles around. There is the concrete driveway with oil stains, and the fuel pump, shaped like a teapot, in front. And out to the side, almost lost to the mangroves crawling up from the creek bed, the remnants of a playground. A swing, its tyre seat hanging low to the ground, where the mangroves, worming unseen, have pushed their stems through the mud.

Do you see the derelict cottage out back? Three sisters live there. Two of them run the roadhouse. Svetlana, the middle sister, waits tables and does the cooking. Oksana, the youngest, works the register and helps with the dishes. The sisters are pale-haired and towering. They wear white blouses, and black pants usually a little too short against their ankles. They keep themselves busy. When the place is empty of custom, Svetlana and Oksana clean the fans and filters above the vats of oil in the kitchen. Scrape the ice from the freezer room walls. Do the book-keeping on one of the diner tables.

Svetlana and Oksana are in the roadhouse now. Cleaning out the cupboards in the kitchen. Spraying for cockroaches. Setting fresh mousetraps. Putting the crockery back. Do you see them in there, under the fluorescent lights, on their knees on the worn linoleum?

And what about the third sister? Tatiana. The eldest. She keeps to the cottage for the most part, though some say they have seen her sitting by the mud and mangroves on the tyre swing in the bruised light of evening, when the crickets begin their chirruping. First one and then suddenly more, you know how it goes, until the air is thick with their din.

A veil, they say, always covers Tatiana's face. Have you heard the rumours? Some say that she is the beautiful one. Her beauty deadly as a siren's. Others that her skin is pocked like the creek mud. That the smell of the creek banks, when the moon sucks the tide away, comes from her mouth. That she summons the clouds of mosquitoes, which swarm up from the marsh when the earth darkens.

It is early afternoon, even though the moon, like a stone, is still visible in the blue sky. The roadhouse looks quiet, but do you see the sign hanging on the inside of the glass door? The place is open for business.

*

Enter another road train, rattling against its chains, crossing the tarmac bridge. This one slowing into the roadhouse driveway. It stops – do you hear with what relief? – by the diesel pump.

Out steps a man with long, uncombed dark hair. Grossly overweight. He strolls the stained concrete with a cigarette in his hand. Surveys the cages stacked on the trailers. Teeming with ugly feathers. Throaty noise. There is the reek of manure, overcoming the tidal odour of the swamp and the stink of fuel.

The truck driver squashes the cigarette underfoot on the concrete, slaps a mosquito that has landed on his hairy hand, and heads inside. There is the surprising sound of the bell as he pushes open the glass door. Like something remembered from childhood.

And there is Oksana, standing erect and solemn behind the counter with its cash register. You can take a look at her now. Taller than the truck driver. Pale-haired. Her colour too wan and her skin too thick for men to believe she is beautiful.

The truck driver winks at Oksana as he passes by, brushing aside the plastic strips hanging in the doorway to the dining room. The ceiling rafters are swathed with a creeper, its foliage thinning, its trunk muscular. There are long windows, framed by curtains of moth-eaten red velveteen. And against the walls are half-a-dozen tables, draped with faded red gingham tablecloths.

The truck driver seats himself at a table by one of the windows, facing the swinging door to the kitchen. There is a fish tank on a stand against the wall there. A goldfish floats on its side in the cloudy water. Can you see it? Playing silently for time, then struggling? The truck driver cannot. Svetlana has already appeared through the swinging door. She stands in front of him, pen and notepad ready.

The truck driver looks up at her pale face. Eyelashes next to invisible. She is almost identical to her younger sister, though she might be taller. Do you agree that there is something clumsier about her?

The fat man's face grows a smile. Svetlana returns the gaze, if not the smile. Seconds pass. The sisters are not known for their conversation. Their skills, people say, are still only rudimentary. The truck driver breaks the silence.

'You don't remember me, do you, love?' He pauses. 'Although I'm fatter. Why not say it? Nothing wrong with talking straight.' He looks at his stomach, covered by a flannel shirt, and pats the fabric there.

The odour of the truck driver's body is mixing with the air. The reek of sweat. Old alcohol. Seeping from his organs, his skin, as if he was pickling himself. Can you smell it? It is hard to tell if

Svetlana does. Standing there in her black pants and white blouse, frilled around the collar. Her hair sprayed into a bun.

The truck driver folds his hands over his swollen belly. Looks up at Svetlana again.

'My dad was always one for straight talking. There was this time when I was a boy. A helicopter crashed on the old farm. Squashed down onto the ground and burst into flames.' The truck driver presses his hands into the yielding flesh of his stomach and then lifts them. Spreads his fingers in the air. Returns his hands to his belly. Looks at them there. 'Afterwards there were these black bodies, out in the paddock, in the long grass. Not that the cows cared.'

Svetlana waits with her notepad and biro. There is a clock ticking. The white one on the wall above the door into the kitchen. The minute hand shudders every time the clock registers the passing of a second.

The fat man looks up at Svetlana again, slowly grinning. 'Well, just before the helicopter came down, as we were watching its death spin from the back porch, Mum turned to Dad and said, *Do something!* Dad said' – and here the truck driver puts on a mock-Italian accent and rhythmically waves his right hand – '*Whadda you want me to do? Catch it?*'

The truck driver stops. His hand is still in the air, and he is smiling up at the tall, thick-skinned woman in front of him. Svetlana looks at him through her pale eyelashes, her pen and notepad poised at chest level. The fat man lowers his hand, smears his sleeve across his mouth. Wiping away the grin. Then he rests his heavy hands on the red-and-white tablecloth, fingers splayed. Begins to inspect them. The nails – perhaps you noticed earlier? – are long and dirty.

'Look, get me a steak, will you? You know how I like it.'

Svetlana brings the notepad and pen close to her face. She scrawls with her blue biro, then walks briskly to the swinging doors, disappearing into the kitchen.

A dry leaf from the vine that clings to the ceiling rafters drifts down to the truck driver's table. Do you see how the creeper appears to be dying in places? Turning crisp and brown. The fat man flicks the curled leaf from the tablecloth onto the floor.

He looks out the long window framed by red velveteen. The swing is there, planted in the earth, just past the edge of the concrete. And the tangle of mangroves, hiding the brown line of the creek. Most of the water drawn out now by the weight of the moon. Can you see the crabs in the mud? Like the skeletons of dolls, crawling silently from grave to grave. And the hovering mosquitoes? The truck driver cannot. He looks up at the moon in the vast plain of the sky.

Into the dining room drifts the sound and smell of cooking steak. Then the fans above the hotplate in the kitchen are switched on. The fat man calls out.

'I'll be right back, love.'

He manoeuvres himself out of his chair and through the plastic strips into the front room. Oksana is gone from behind the counter there. The bell rings as he opens the door and steps out onto the concrete driveway, suddenly bright. He shields his eyes and heads for the fuel pump and the truck.

The chickens sound dusty. Their throats. Claws. Wings. Feathers in the dark cages. Can you hear them? The truck driver hears nothing. He swings open the door of the cabin. Tucks his long greasy hair behind one ear and leans down to the polystyrene box he keeps on the floor to retrieve a tepid can of beer.

Look quickly: up there! A pelican flying across the highway. From the direction of the museum. Beating the air with its wings as if its soul was old and heavy. It flaps over the semitrailer, circles over the roadhouse. Floats down to rest, flapping and grabbing with its claws at the frame of the old swing. The bird clutches the rusted steel, fluffs its wings and sinks its gullet into the rancid feathers on its chest. Blinks its eyes, rimmed like targets.

From there, the pelican watches the truck driver. The fat man slams the door of his truck. Opens the can. After a sharp crack the tin makes another noise. Like the truck did – do you remember? A sound of release.

The truck driver makes his way back to the roadhouse. Pushes open the glass door, once again triggering that small bell. Thrusts aside the plastic strips to the dining room and sees, on the checked cloth of his table, a brown steak on a plate with a pile of yellow chips. All framed by the curtains of red velveteen, eaten by moths and silverfish over who knows how many years. How long do they say that the three sisters have been here?

The truck driver sits down on his chair. Svetlana is nowhere to be seen. He takes a drink of his beer and puts the can down. Picks up his knife and fork. Pulls his chair in. Starts sawing off a portion of the T-bone steak, brown juice and oil mixing on his plate.

Do you see that the fish in the glass tank has stopped moving? It floats now, waterlogged. Just below the surface. The truck driver, busy with his food, does not notice.

*

Enter an old white ute in the driveway of the roadhouse. Watch its slow approach through the windows of the dining room. The truck driver, chewing a piece of steak, watches it too. The ute comes to a stop just outside his window. In a spot near the swing, where the concrete of the roadhouse merges with the mud and the mangroves. And then, further below, the creek bed, crabs clawing their way out of muddy holes. The brown line of water. Soundless clouds of mosquitoes.

Can you see that the pelican, roosting on top of the abandoned swing, has turned its attention to the car? There is the squawk of the door, all stiff around its edges, and an old man emerges. Thin, with bandy legs. He leans on a cane. Closes the car door, which creaks, then bangs. Pats the dog tied by a rope on the ute's tray. The old Labrador, fur like a doormat, thumps its tail.

The old man walks around to the roadhouse door. There is the tinkle of the bell, again like a reminder of something, and then he is inside. Oksana appears at the front counter – did you see her there just briefly? – but retreats as the old man heads towards the dining room. He pushes through the plastic strips with his cane. Walks past the truck driver and sits down at a table ahead of him. Notice how the old man is too polite to sit with his back to the other fellow? The truck driver, though, keeps busy with his steak.

The old man looks through the window between the tattered drapes to his dog outside. He notices the pelican, like a creature from another world, roosting on top of the derelict swing. Then Svetlana is there, pale and large, like the bird, standing at his other side. The old man looks up at her with watery eyes. Speaks softly.

'Oh, hello there, young lady. Steak and chips, please.'

Do you notice how his head rocks slightly? How he holds onto the walking stick, which he has laid on the gingham tablecloth in front of him, his hands mottled and jittery? Svetlana pays no heed to these signs of age. She scrawls on her notepad with her biro. Holding it close to her nose. Then she bustles off, bun firm on the top of her head. The hems of her black pants hectic around her ankles. She disappears through the swinging door. A leaf from the vine on the ceiling floats to the floor.

Now the truck driver, still chewing and holding his cutlery ready, regards the newcomer at the table ahead of him. The old man is watching his own fingers. Do you see how they look? Bony and unsettled, like crabs, on the wood of the cane. The fat man, swallowing his steak, decides to intervene.

'You're English, then. Still got quite an accent.'

The old man looks up at the bloated face of the truck driver, framed in uncombed hair, and then down again at his fingers on the walking stick. The wood of the cane is old and dull.

'Yes, yes,' he says, 'fair enough. Well, Welsh, actually, but yes, yes.'

Like the truck driver, the old man has yet to notice the fish tank on the nearby wall. The dead fish now belly-up against a corner. Do you see it there? Washed out and swollen. Pressed against the glass. As if something – the wind, a tide – had pushed it into that place.

The truck driver, without putting down his cutlery, wipes his mouth on his flannel sleeve. 'My dad had an accent.'

The old man, quaint in his manners, dutifully looks up from his cane. He has a blanched face and moist eyes. The truck driver, knife and fork in hand, slowly grins at him. The same grin he gave Svetlana.

'One time, when I was a kid, a couple of Jehovah's Witnesses came to the door. Two old birds. You know the type I mean. Dad was yelling at them, and the old birds looked all confused. They asked: *Why don't we go out with our wives?* Then Dad yelled louder' – and here the truck driver mocks an Italian accent again, performing flourishes with the knife in his right hand – '*No, I said, Why don'ta you get on with your lives?*'

The old man looks down at his cane. Scrawny hands curled over the stick. There is the sound and smell of frying steak. The fans in the kitchen go back on. And can you hear the chips spitting in the oil?

The fat man's smile fades. He lowers his knife and studies his plate. There is a little meat left, hard up against the pale curvature of the bone. The truck driver stabs a chip with the fork in his left hand and stuffs it into his mouth. Suddenly the old man speaks.

'Oh, my wife has been dead for years.'

Now the dog outside the roadhouse starts to bark. The noise grows. Becomes relentless as a machine. The truck driver and the old man look through their windows framed in that old red velveteen. Can you see what has happened? The Labrador has finally noticed the pelican. It reverses on the tray to get a better view of the bird over the roof of the ute. The rope tied to its neck stretches, grows taut. Do you see how the dog's belly contracts with every noise? And do you hear how with each bark, austere as a gunshot, there is an echo? The noise ricocheting between the mangroves and the roadhouse wall. And listen: there is another noise. In the clamour, the chickens, hidden within the dark cages on the semitrailer, are beginning to stir.

The pelican stretches its neck, jowl emerging from the oily feathers on its sternum. It looks first to the mangroves. The pocked banks of the creek. The crabs slipping back into their lairs beneath the mud. The brown water from the tide – coming back in now, do you see it? – trickling in after them. Then the bird turns to regard the barking dog.

Inside the roadhouse Svetlana emerges from the swinging doors with another T-bone and a pile of fat chips. The old man turns away from the window. He makes room on his table. Lays the cane across his lap, still holding onto it. Svetlana places the dish on the checked tablecloth, along with cutlery wrapped in a paper napkin, skin-tight. She starts to move away, but the old man stops her.

'Could you cut the steak for me, please, young lady?'

The old man makes a tutting sound, looking down at the plate. Shaking his head. Svetlana unscrolls the knife and fork in a single movement. Lays the curled napkin on the table. Pulls the plate towards her and, hunched over her work, begins carving the steak. Rigorously skinning the meat from the bone, where there is still blood. Then dicing up the slab of cooked steak. The dog outside keeps barking.

Suddenly there is an alien noise. Inside the dining room. Can you hear it? Wheezing. No. Weeping. It is the old man. Head down to his chest. Look: his shoulders are shaking.

Svetlana abruptly stops cutting. Stands up from the plate, cutlery still in her hands. A morsel of brown meat falls onto the worn carpet. Svetlana does not see it. Instead she sees, through the window between the ragged curtains, the barking dog on the back of the ute. And the pelican on the top of the swing. Do you see it there too? Its head high. Its gullet bulging. Its wings spread as if for flight. Dripping greasy feathers from their undersides.

*

Now it is evening. The sky bleeds all the way to the horizon. The frogs, lying in the marshlands, are sending their echoes. The crickets join in. See how the clouds of mosquitoes are beginning to rise as the earth turns to the night? To the never-ending blackness of the universe, where they say that everything – even all of this – began? And look: here come the starlings. One. Three. A dozen or more. Sweeping through the insects. Their noise shrill as panic. Their tiny hearts like ticking bombs.

The highway is black and silent. Beneath the bridge the creek is full, the water still as mud amid the mangroves. The museum is empty and dark. Across the tarmac road, the sign on the glass of the roadhouse door reads CLOSED.

But look! Tatiana is there on the tyre swing. Gently rocking. Her feet on the earth, among the shoots of the mangroves probing their way unseen through the mud. She wears black pants, like her sisters. But, as legend has it, her veil is on. There is no breeze to lift it. Can you see how impossible it is, in this shiftless place, to glimpse her face, to get a proper look?

Let us leave her. Look to the marshlands that open up just beyond the concrete driveway and the white roadhouse with its cottage out the back. A flock of ibises has appeared there in the swamp grass. Against the evening light. The silhouettes of their black heads like pickaxes.

DOUBLING UP: FINDING INSPIRATION IN LIFE AND LITERATURE

essay by Maria Takolander

Consider, for a moment, the thrill of reading fiction. You are transported to a different place, time or being. Absorbed in the story, you are somewhere else, someone else, seeing a different – sometimes uplifting, sometimes uncomfortable – vision of things. Nevertheless, the experience is always ultimately about the nonfictional you. It is about what you bring back from the reading: how it affects your mood; how it shifts your understanding of yourself and your world; how it makes you see or dream anew. In that way every reader engages in a highly individual creative act: re-envisioning his or her relationship with the world in terms of the patterns offered by literature. When a reader transcribes that vision into words, he or she becomes a writer.

That is how I see what I do. A lifetime of reading has shown me how I might write; that is, how I might transform the chaotic flux of my life into something with potential significance. Thus the act of writing always involves a doubling up of inspiration: life and literature enfold and interpenetrate.

'Three Sisters' – the subject of this commentary – foregrounds this creative doubleness. The story is based, in part, on my experience of working in a roadhouse in Tooradin, a swampy town in Southwest Gippsland in Victoria, with three sisters of Dutch origin. In that way, the story finds its inspiration in life. However, this story also acknowledges Anton Chekhov's famous play of the same name, which made my autobiographical experience of working with three sisters so distinctive and potentially poignant to me in the first place. My story, calling itself after Chekhov's *Three Sisters*, identifies its primary source of inspiration in literature.

*

To explain my philosophy of writing further, let me take you back to my years as an undergraduate student. Gerald Murnane was my fiction tutor at Victoria College in Toorak in the early 1990s, and he was always encouraging us to 'write what you know'. It was his mantra.

To begin with, I ignored him. The first story I wrote was about a paedophilic priest. Gerald accused the story of being 'topical', by which I assume he meant inauthentic and exploitative. However, he did identify the only passage in the story based on personal experience. After that, despite being stung by his criticism, I was convinced that Gerald had preternatural powers. For my next story I wrote an autobiographical piece, which was what I mistakenly thought Gerald wanted when he induced me to 'write what I know'. Naïve and narcissistic, I thought that I must be of inherent interest; I thought that it was the secret truth of me that was being sought. When the story was workshopped in class, Gerald was lukewarm in his response. More to the point, my fellow students did not seem to care for what I had written; no one believed in the meaningfulness of the material that I had drawn directly from my life.

I continue to 'write what I know', although now that category is broadly conceived. My writing is informed by places I have inhabited, people I have encountered, stories I have been told, films I have watched, emotional states I have experienced, ideas that have captured my interest, situations I have witnessed, and events that have happened to me. There is indeed a lot that an individual person might 'know' – and write about with the kind of attachment that can pass for authority. However, I write with the recognition that my autobiographical experience is not *ipso facto* interesting; it is not readymade literature. That material has to be forged into fiction; that is, transformed into something that will engage a reader's sense of meaningfulness. It has to be selected, elaborated on and crafted with a view to creating narrative, significance and ambiguity.

In other words, to write successfully, I have to read life in the way that I have learnt to read literature, intuiting and identifying prospectively interesting characters, evocative settings and powerful themes. It is a practice that requires a certain distance from one's experience – in the way that carrying a camera does, as one continually thinks about what might be photographed and how best to frame subjects. However, it is also a practice that requires an understanding of the appropriate and successful conventions for choosing and representing material. In this way, the activity of reading becomes of paramount importance to the ability to write, so much so that while it could be said that I 'write what I know', it could also be said that I 'write what I read'.

*

I would like to spend a little more time elaborating on what it means to be a reader – and then on what it means to be a writer. I have always been a voracious reader, which means that I have always lived in a world reverberating with the characters, symbols, settings and dilemmas provided by books. That world, unlike the material one, is infinitely rich with meaning – inclusive even of meaninglessness – and further enriched with every great book I read.

In a way, literature is like a religion that provides me with an imaginary landscape to inhabit. That imaginary landscape runs parallel to my material one; or perhaps it is truer to say that my material environment is resonantly overlain with the meanings provided by the imaginary one. However, perhaps less like religion, literature provides me with an imaginary world that is open and inexhaustible, always provoking me to consider different ways of thinking and being. Sometimes I feel located and comforted by a book: at other times profoundly dislocated and discomfited. However, I always feel intensely engaged with the world in which I live.

That sense of engagement with life is forged through the imaginative transactions with the world that books continually encourage me to make. The world, literature tells me as a reader, is not given; it is there for me to think about and to meaningfully, or playfully, re-create.

In *Art Objects: Essays on Ecstasy and Effrontery*, the writer Jeanette Winterson addresses how reading literature can be thrilling and confronting precisely because it is constantly changing us and challenging our hold on things. 'Mostly,' she writes, 'we work hard at taming our … environment.' Indeed, many people don't read, or they read genre formats that won't unsettle them with new patterns of meaning. However, for Winterson, symbolically endangering ourselves via imaginative experience is important. If we hide from the risks of literature, we risk letting a small body of stories, as Winterson puts it, rust into our flesh. If we read widely and boldly, we inhabit what Winterson memorably describes as 'energetic space'.

That 'energetic space' is the space in which we, as readers, continually and creatively rethink our lives in the light of literature's grappling with the human condition. If we, as readers, put the proverbial pen to paper, that 'energetic space' also gives rise to writing.

*

Writing, thus conceived, is an intensely readerly activity. Yet there exists significant anxiety about the practice of writers reading. Contextualising creativity, acknowledging the powerful tradition of literature out of which every writer writes, inspires fears of plagiarism and unoriginality.

The literary critic Harold Bloom famously gave expression to such concerns in *The Anxiety of Influence*, in which he represents writers struggling against their literary precursors to achieve independence. I don't experience writing in this way, and I believe that an antagonistic position vis-à-vis literary predecessors is unnecessary, especially if one reads – to re-appropriate Winterson's word – energetically.

It is also the case that each of us lives an individual life, so that a single book marks each of us differently. It is probably impossible to read – and write – the same piece of literature twice, as the Argentine writer Jorge Luis Borges comically suggests in 'Pierre Menard, Author of the Quixote'. In this short story, a fictional twentieth-century French author called Menard re-creates an identical, but also richer, version of Miguel de Cervantes' classic seventeenth-century Spanish novel *Don Quixote*. After Borges, Italo Calvino's novel *If on a Winter's Night a Traveller* portrays a character copying out parts of Fyodor Dostoevsky's *Crime and Punishment*.

I have heard students profess that they avoid reading in order to maintain an original voice. Such a hostile stance to literary tradition is counterproductive. As the literary critic Mustapha Marrouchi argues, our reading, 'from pre-school nursery rhymes to high school Shakespeare and university Milton provides us with the keys to nearly all the imaginative experience that it is possible for us to have in life'. Reading also provides us with the keys to imagining the unique experience of our lives. That is to say, reading the work of others ironically teaches us how we might write our own original stories.

*

'Three Sisters', most clearly in its title, explicitly acknowledges the ways in which I was mindful of Chekhov's *Three Sisters* when I wrote my story – just as the lives of the three Brontë sisters are said to have been on Chekhov's mind when he wrote his play. Chekhov's text, as I have suggested, provided me with the vision necessary to identify my life experience of working in a roadhouse with three sisters as potential literature. It also provided a prevailing mood for my fictional transformation of the autobiographical material.

Chekhov's play is marked by an exquisite sense of loneliness and nostalgia: the three sisters and other characters in Chekhov's text constantly long for another time and place. Likewise, the three sisters in my story are displaced and foreign, although it is the other characters – the men who visit the roadhouse – who express their isolation and despair. Chekhov's play provides the impression of seasonal change and an image of migrating birds, thereby suggesting a natural environment that is vast and free, as well as profoundly indifferent to the small and melancholy conditions of the characters' lives. Similarly, my story draws attention to the inhuman environment – the tide, crickets, crabs, bird life – that continues outside the roadhouse, mindless of the pathetic human dramas played out inside. Indeed, staging events much like a play, my story insists that attention be paid to such things. Evoking pantomime, my story attempts to directly engage readers, prompting them to heed certain elements of each scene.

However, my story probably hinges most on a line delivered by the elderly doctor in Chekhov's work: 'Perhaps I'm not really a man, and am only pretending that I've got arms and legs and a head; perhaps I don't exist at all, and only imagine that I walk, and eat, and sleep.' It is a sentiment that has always stayed with me, in part because it coincides with similar sentiments absorbed from other texts – such as Shakespeare's *Macbeth* ('Life's but a walking shadow, a poor player') or Beckett's *Waiting for Godot* – which have collectively attuned me to the brevity and unreality of the lives we lead in the measureless and otherworldly context of time and space. There is something profoundly alien about us. This theme has become something of an obsession for me.

My story does not rehearse Chekhov's play – and it was never in any danger of doing so. My life experience in late twentieth-century rural Australia was very different from Chekhov's experience of nineteenth-century and early twentieth-century Russia. As an 'energetic' reader, my writing is also influenced by more than Chekhov's play. It is inspired by literature that has long explored the human condition of melancholy estrangement, as well as by a haunting cross-cultural tradition that mobilises the mythic trope of the three sisters.

Nevertheless, without Chekhov's play, would I have been inspired to conceptualise my prosaic experience of working in a roadhouse as the material for a short story? The answer is no. We write in an echo chamber, as fiction such as Borges' and Calvino's reminds us, reverberating with the stories of other writers that have come before us. And that's okay. In fact, it provides the enriched experience of being alive that we, as readers and writers, look to literature for in the first place.

Bibliography

Bloom, H. 1973 *The Anxiety of Influence: A Theory of Poetry*, Oxford University Press, New York.

Chekhov, A. 1983 (1901) *Three Sisters*, trans. Michael Frayn, Methuen, London.

Mustapha, M. 2006, 'The Value of Literature as Public Institution', *College Literature* 33.4, pp120-197.

Winterson, J. 1996 *Art Objects: Essays on Ecstasy and Effrontery*. Alfred A. Knopf, New York.

BU 33 ZU
NEW SOUTH WALES

'WHAT I DIDN'T PUT IN MY SPEECH'

Claire Aman

After my speech at Davey's wedding, I head for the drinks table in a way that could only be described as agricultural. Davey's backyard is steep. I've got my elbows out and my legs are like cranks. Heavy duty, that's me these days. I think everyone liked the speech. They're smiling and clapping anyway. Davey and his bride are perfect on the verandah, like on a wedding cake. Nothing could be finer.

Up at the drinks table it's help yourself. I pull a beer out of the bathtub ice. Davey's old friend Leo Addicoat takes the bottle from my fingers, twists off the top and hands it back to me. A pink hibiscus flops to and fro in his hatband as he moves his head. He looks like Leonard Cohen in that hat. I bet he's going bald. I haven't seen him for years. Davey and Leo used to share a house in the early eighties, when Davey first moved here to Sydney.

There's a woman next to him. She's fluttering a Chinese fan in tight little movements. He introduces me. 'This is Davey's cousin, Judith,' he tells her. 'Stunning speech, Judith,' she says to me, and her lips form a red smile. She tells me she didn't know Davey used to be reckless. 'I never knew he had that terrible fall,' she says.

Other people are touching my shoulder now. 'From Plumbago,' I tell them. 'On the north coast.'

'Is that anywhere near Byron?' someone asks. I suck on the bottle and the beer comes fizzing out in a rush, all over my dress.

'Steady,' says Leo. He takes a handful of purple serviettes from the table and dabs at me.

'Life's reckless,' I say. But the woman with the Chinese fan has forgotten me. She's turned to face the verandah. Now the bride's father is talking. It's starting to get dark and he's holding his speech up close to his face. He talks on and on about his daughter.

I decide to share a secret with Leo Addicoat.

'I saved his life,' I whisper, looking straight ahead.

'Who?' says Leo.

'Me and Jim Morrison,' I say, but Leo has pushed his hands into the bathtub and is fishing around for bottles. He opens a dark ale and puts his cold fingertips on my neck. 'Will you sing for us tonight, Jude?'

'No way,' I tell him. Haven't sung for years.

I'm in a sweat from toiling up the garden so I wipe some ice over my cheeks. This dress is too tight around my armpits. There's a can of bourbon and coke winking at me from the bathtub and I can't resist it. What the hell. My duties are done.

Because I don't know most of the guests, I've spent the afternoon standing around with Leo. Davey and his new bride certainly have a lot of friends. Davey's lived in Sydney for thirty years now. He hasn't been back to Plumbago since his dad, my Uncle Frank, died. Because us Hartigans are chronically prone to death and feuds, it turned out that I was the one and only family member coming to the wedding. That's why I got to make the speech.

I thought Leo would have made the speech. He and Davey go back a long way. I used to catch the train down from Plumbago to Sydney and stay at their place. They rented an old house in Ashfield, in a street called Palace Street. It was all sofas and bongs and flagons and the stereo full blast. Or we'd get stoned and drive to Stanwell Park in Davey's Torana and listen to Pink Floyd or

The Doors while we waited for the sun to come up. We liked our music. I knew how to belt out a song when I was young. And Leo thought he could play guitar.

Leo used to be a sweetheart. You could trust him. One night I got into his bed. He'd gone out with a girl and Davey thought he wouldn't come home. I pretended to be asleep when he came in. I remember how he lay down with his head at the other end of the bed. Top to tail like children.

Now I ask him if he remembers Davey's Torana.

He remembers. 'Apache Red. Globe mags, triple side-draft Stromberg carbies, extractors and a two inch exhaust. God, that thing was a hottie. Davey used to tell everyone Torana was Aboriginal for flying.'

'I'm the only person I know who learnt to drive in a V8 Holden piranha,' I say. Leo's still got that cackling laugh.

'We were off our heads back then,' he says. 'Lucky no one got killed.'

'Yeah,' I say. 'Lucky.'

Back then Leo had been saving up to go to Europe. He was in Paris when Davey fell. By the time he came back three years later, everything had been put right. I haven't seen him since Palace Street. He was Davey's friend.

Yes, but there are things Leo doesn't know.

I tell him he looks like Leonard Cohen. He takes the hat off. Yep, he's got a bald patch. I knew it.

Then I ask him, 'Remember the stereo in that car?'

'I'll never forget that stereo,' says Leo. 'Remember the graphic equaliser? All those knobs?'

It's cooling down. The weather has been unstable all day. We've had two squalls that sent us all running to the gazebos, followed by dazzling sunshine. 'It's more like Melbourne than Sydney,' says Leo, and he goes to put his jacket on. When he misses the armhole and catches his arm, he gives me a comical, helpless look. He hasn't changed. I would have pretended it wasn't happening. I help him with the sleeve.

The lipsticked one's wandered off. I ask him who she was. From Davey's work, he says. Nice, I say. He says yeah, no, sort of, and he scans the crowd. I think he could be lonely with his bald patch, so I haven't asked him if he has anyone.

'I hope it works out for Davey this time,' I say. This is Davey's third wedding. He and Christine have stepped off the verandah into a sea of wedding guests. Everyone wants to hug them. Davey's so tall his head rises above everyone else's. Christine's white dress appears and disappears as the crowd tosses this way and that. I've hardly had a chance to talk to Davey all afternoon.

I only arrived last night. Davey paid for my ticket. I practised my speech to myself on the plane, looking out of the window. Down below was tufty with puckers and folds – gold, chocolate and watermelon green with twisty rivers. But as we neared Sydney it all disappeared and there was only cloud. We went bumping through the big white nothing towards the ground, and I thought the plane would shake itself apart and I would die by falling.

Later in the cab I remembered that when a person falls, they can appear – from above – like a leaf dropping. I've pictured it thousands of times. On a humid Sunday in 1983 I watched Davey fall backwards off a rock face in Sherwood National Park. He lay slow in the air with his arms and legs spread out, looking up at the sky. He did a sort of double-take when he landed, like a bounce. Then he lay frozen in the same position, arms and legs out, face up. Don't move, I yelled. I didn't mean for Davey not to move. The truth is I was yelling at the universe to stop. Like that poem at school about pulling the sun in. Turn out the stars, take everything down. Davey's gone.

'Hope he gets it together this time,' I say to Leo, and we clink our drinks together.

Men fall. They think they're invincible. They get this mad gleam and next thing they're balancing on the very edge of a cliff, pissing themselves laughing. Then we have to look after them when they land on their heads. But even though I'm a female, I know what that crazy light feels like. I had it after Davey fell. The difference is, I used it to save his life.

This is what Leo Addicoat doesn't know: Davey wouldn't be here today if it wasn't for me.

Davey and Christine are dancing. It's meant to be romantic but the ground is so steep, and he's pumping her arm up and down and they're laughing. It's been a long afternoon and I've eaten too many smoked oysters. Times like this I feel like a cigarette but I can't see any smokers. Everyone's given up. A girl tugs her boyfriend to his feet for a dance, so we nab their chairs. He gives us a dirty look over her shoulder as they shamble past. I tip the last of my bourbon down my throat.

Leo sits with his knees together and his feet apart, toes turned in. He leans forwards and studies me.

'You and Davey are getting more alike,' he says. 'Except for your eyes.'

It's hard to know in a small family like ours. Davey's eyes are dark and abrupt. I don't know where he got them.

I wonder if I can trust Leo not to laugh at me. I test him out. 'Did Davey ever tell you we had three great uncles in Scotland who got killed on their way home from a wedding?'

I've seen a photo taken at the wedding: doomed and bright, they raise their glasses and grin.

'No,' says Leo.

'They drove off a bridge,' I say. 'When we were kids.'

They drowned before I ever got to meet them, those old men with their plaid waistcoats and shining bald heads.

I tell him about my family's pig theory. 'My grandmother said it was bad luck if you see a pig on your way to a wedding. They must have seen a pig.'

I check he's trying not to laugh, but he just leans on his elbow and rests his chin on his thumb, curling his forefinger around his nose.

'Lucky you came by plane, Jude,' he says.

I never talk about it, but I changed after Davey fell. I became like the great uncles with those superstitious grins splitting their faces. Ever since he fell I've been kind of in mid-air myself. Relationships blow up, jobs fall through, nothing holds.

I maintain my direction. 'It was weird when Davey fell.'

'Shock to the system,' he says. 'How old would you have been then?'

'Twenty-two. The rock ledge broke off.'

I sprinted all the way through the bush to the car park. I never knew I could run so fast. I thought Davey was dead. I had to show the rescue team where he was. The ambulance took him to Plumbago Hospital but the doctors took one look and flew him to Sydney.

'Horrific,' says Leo. He looks into my eyes.

I tell him I still hate the sound of bellbirds. He hands me another bourbon.

'It was weird when he was in hospital,' I say. 'You're not supposed to be full of beans when your cousin's in a coma.'

'What do you mean full of beans?' he says.

'I don't know.' A girl offers us a platter of potato chips. We grab up big handfuls.

'I drove Davey's Torana down to Sydney,' I say. 'I couldn't leave it up at Sherwood, he would have murdered me. I got his car keys out of his backpack.'

'Where did you stay?'

'Palace Street, in your old room. My uncle and aunt stayed at the house too. They drove down from Plumbago. They sat in the kitchen crying. I didn't know what to do.'

'I wish I'd been around to help,' he says.

'I held out my stupid hand to stop him.' Couldn't catch him.

'Nothing you could do,' says Leo.

'Everything went out of balance. I lost my job but I didn't care. I just wanted him to wake up. I went to the hospital every night. My uncle and aunt spent every day there with him and I did the night shift. All the nurses knew me. I sat at the window, I didn't want him to think I was staring at him while he was in bed. All his tubes. Yeah, and I was worried about tripping over some piece of medical shit and the whole thing going defunct.'

'Look at him now though,' says Leo. 'You'd never know. He was lucky, no damage.'

I didn't put this in my speech, but I'm the reason Davey survived. Me and Jim Morrison. Every night while he was in the coma, I drove his Torana really fast to his favourite song.

Davey was on the seventh floor of the Royal Prince Alfred Hospital, in room five. The song 'Roadhouse Blues' goes for four minutes and four seconds. The fastest I drove Davey's Torana was a hundred and eighty kilometres an hour. Someone had to do it.

I put it like this to Leo, and as I career through, I'm sleek and shiny and the wild uncle grin is spreading over my face. See, I got this idea that if I went fast enough, Davey would wake up. Every night when I left the hospital I'd get on the expressway in that red car of his. Do you remember how 'Roadhouse Blues' starts? Thunka-thunka-thunka-diggerdy, thunka-thunka-thunka-diggerdy, then Morrison gives a shout. I'd get a bit of speed up, then I'd peg it back a couple of gears and plant my foot. *Keep your eyes on the road, your hands upon the whee-el.* That thing was a rocket. If this, then that. One night I did a hundred and fifty. Next day his toe twitched. I raced for him. He moved a finger. I kept it up. Faster every night. One time I switched the headlights off. Talk about sick joy. The next day Davey had a little smile. I did it every night until he woke up. The night he opened his eyes I stopped fanging his car. Gravity, velocity, stability. 'Look at him now,' I say. 'Jim Morrison's been dead for forty-two years. You work it out, Leo.'

The first star has come out. Everyone is dancing now, with Davey and Christine in the middle. Leo Addicoat puts his arms around me.

'Don't ever say anything to Davey,' I tell him. Leo shakes his head. 'Love ya, Judy Blue-eyes,' he says. I smile up at him, and in a way that I, at any rate, would describe as poetry in motion, we dance.

DAYDREAMING IS NEVER A WASTE OF TIME

essay by Claire Aman

Weddings are highly charged. Everyone's dressed up, there's love, family, drinking and dancing. There are people you haven't seen for years. It's tempting to get things off your chest. Every time I go to a wedding I come home with something that finds its way into a story.

'What I Didn't Put in My Speech' is not factual. At the same time, it's about things I've experienced and which have affected me. So while it's not factual, it's still true.

The plot didn't happen. I've never raced a car believing it would wake anyone out of a coma. I didn't have a cousin who fell off a cliff, or even a cousin to visit. My great-uncles didn't die in a car crash. My family is not superstitious or prone to death and feuds. I don't like bourbon and I never could sing.

What is factual though, is that my brother survived a coma years ago, and I spent a lot of time with him at the hospital. It's also true that I made a speech at another brother's wedding, and I practised my speech while looking out of an aeroplane, hoping we wouldn't crash. It's true that I saw a friend of mine fall off a small cliff. Luckily, he's alright. It's true that I had three Scottish great-uncles. I have a photo of them. True, I lived in share houses in the eighties and yes, we had fancy car stereos. I still listen to The

Doors. These unrelated things are all facts. But I didn't want to write an account of my brother's coma, or my friend's fall, or my great-uncles' lives. I write fiction.

As well as the facts, there's another class of truths. They include recollected emotions, resonant images and thoughts that hang around unreasonably. They're probably daydreams.

> At my brother's wedding, I felt for a moment the effort of walking uphill as somehow agricultural, as if I was a tractor.
>
> When I thought of my friend falling, my recollection was that he fell face up, looking up at the sky (he thinks he fell face down).
>
> When I look at my great-uncles in the photo, I see grinning, bewitched-looking, superstitious men.
>
> A man I know, after escaping with burns from an explosion, bought a powerful car. As he showed us the car, I noticed his huge reckless smile. His wife said he had been different since the explosion.
>
> After looking down from a tall building in Melbourne, I kept thinking about gravity.
>
> From an aeroplane, the ground reminded me of my grandfather's bedspread, with squares of furrowed paddocks.
>
> Later on the same flight, we flew into cloud, and I was scared of falling.
>
> A woman I know said as we parted after chatting in the street: *your destiny comes to meet you*, and I imagined destiny as the ground rushing up.

These unconnected recurring daydreamed truths appealed to me. After a while they felt like pieces of something.

When my daydreams feel like they are becoming something, I buy a black spiral-bound art notebook with thick white unlined pages. The notebook is not for 'material', it's for recording the thought process for a particular story. In the notebook for this story there are pages of incoherent notes. There are descriptions of football matches, car races, views from aeroplanes. There are lots of sentences beginning *Ever since you fell…* There's a list of Torana colours, notes about Leo, pages of *That's why I stole the car. No. It's my car. It's your car. You're my cousin. No you're not.* I never cross anything out. There are lots of questions. It's one notebook, one story, one at a time. The notebook contains the story I'm thinking about. Ideas don't get tangled up or leak into future stories. When the story's finished the notebook's over.

The story took seven months. For five months I didn't know what it was about. It originated when my friend fell in June 2012. I started thinking about gravity, and I realised I was going to write about someone falling. Two months later I bought the notebook.

I wrote down those thoughts that were loitering in my imagination – my friend falling backwards, the agricultural look of my grandfather's old bedspread, my fear in the plane, the smile of the man with his fast car. I glued in a picture of the view from a tall building. The words about *your destiny coming to meet you* had their own page.

These things became the bones of the story, although I had no story in mind when I wrote them down.

I was a long way from having a story. A plot was the last thing I had.

In Melbourne, my father told me *don't fall* as I was leaving on my motorbike. I told him he shouldn't fall either, and my hand hovered, as if it would magically catch him. I noted that superstitious hand.

I watched the football and made notes about how those reckless men weren't afraid of falling over. I wrote notes about men and their risks and spills. It all fitted. I thought more about my long-dead grandfather.

In October, a thought came from nowhere: *It's not you that's reckless, it's life.* I wrote it down. I watched motorcar racing. It made me remember young guys I used to know, and their hotted up cars, and their faces when they drove. I scribbled about them in long sentences with bad spelling.

I still had no idea where the story was going, but I knew for certain it was alive. It had developed a magnetic field. Images and ideas were gravitating towards it. Everything was significant. Nothing was irrelevant. Although the lack of plot gave me a kind of hungry sensation, I tried not to worry. It happens every time.

I happened to watch the film *Chariots of Fire*. The main character says when he is running fast he can feel God's pleasure. It was akin to a rapture. I thought again about the reckless boys in cars, their mad, bright smiles. I looked at the photo again. My great-uncles were my grandfather's brothers. I never met them. I wrote in my notebook that they were glad-eyed, mad-eyed men. I wrote the word fey. Just now I looked it up in the dictionary. It means other-worldly, whimsical, fated to die soon. This is why I love the mystery of writing.

Around November, something changed. I wrote in my notebook: *Ever since he fell, I've been wanting to go fast, do some crazy breakneck thing.* I didn't know who would say this, or why. But I was getting a plot. It was hard to see where to go. Who was this person wanting to go fast? Who fell? This person had changed since somebody fell. He'd become like the great-uncles with the mad gleam. But there had to be more.

I decided the person who'd fallen was in a coma. But who were they, what had happened, and what would happen next?

It seems that the more I interrogate a story, the less it wants to tell me. I have to come at it sideways.

I wondered, what was the name of the person who fell? After sleeping on this, I decided it was Davey. Davey was the son of family friends when we were children. I remember him as a three-year-old bursting away from the adults and running towards the sea. The mind supplies answers. Davey is linked with family and the past, and he's reckless. I recalled his eyes.

Now I knew Davey, I could see him as a daredevil on the edge of the cliff. I made him fall.

I started using a more confident hand in my notebook: *Ever since Davey fell I've been a different person. I'm driving too fast on the way to the hospital. One day I see his finger move. Last night I went 130 kph. When he wakes up, I slow down.* The person in this story would bargain for Davey waking up by driving fast. At last, I was on firm ground with the plot.

But who was behind the wheel? Maybe a cousin. Not a brother or sister. The story was certainly about family, but I didn't want to write about my brother's coma. Male or female cousin? How old? What car? When is all this happening, anyway?

I distracted myself by researching the brain. This didn't add anything to the story. I already knew that it was useful to sit with a person in a coma. My character didn't want to stare at Davey and his tubes. That was all I knew.

By December, I was tired of searching for Davey's diffident cousin. One night I put on The Doors' 'Roadhouse Blues' and listened to the muscular bass and galloping piano. I made notes: *Thunka thunka thunka diggerdy, thunka thunka thunka diggerdy.* The song has a reckless, driving sound. It reminds me of the seventies. I went back to my story with an era and a soundtrack. This is the story's energy.

In January, I gave a speech at my brother's wedding. Leaving the wedding that night, I noticed my toiling walk. It went in the notebook. *I flail up the hill, nothing so much as agriculturally – like a tractor.* Suddenly I'd caught my character, the one who would drive too fast with the mad grin. To my surprise she was a woman my age at a wedding after making a speech. And there I'd been, thinking it was about men.

In my mind, this character was telling someone about how she saved Davey. Who could she tell? After my brother's wedding I made up Leo Addicoat – someone you meet at a wedding that you haven't seen for ages. I thought he should be kind-hearted, so the narrator would trust him with her secret. I got his innocent body language from watching a man in a meeting. I'm always watching.

The last thing I gathered in was an honoured place in the story for the smiling great-uncles. I've always liked their photo. I researched Scottish superstitions and discovered the belief about what happens if you see a pig on your way to a wedding. Here was a role for them. I made them fey, without knowing what that meant. I hope they wouldn't have minded. Their presence brings together family, superstition, a wedding, an accident and the grin of the reckless. It's also a way for Judy to test whether she can trust Leo to take her seriously.

*

My husband is my muse. He provided the core notion to the story: that humans are seekers of meaning. Humans like to attach significance to events, objects and actions. We try to control things by using rituals, like Judy speeding in the Torana. While I'm not superstitious, I can easily imagine believing that if I drove fast I could change the future. It would be great if we could. I can feel that mad smile spreading over my face right now.

I haven't been trained in writing, and I feel my way in the dark. I've noticed that the longer and richer the early imprecise, dream-like, garnering, unassuming stage lasts, the easier it will be for me to eventually sit and write the story. It's as if my subconscious needs to be fed before it will throw me a plot. I just have to trust it wasn't a waste of time. Everything eventually finds its right place in the story. I can't spontaneously make up a plot. My subconscious seems to be in charge of choosing images, orienting them, and stringing them together. The notebook is essential. When everything is finally ready, I see the beginnings of a story. Then I slowly unearth it, using the now-harmonious images and notions I've scribbled in my notebook. Then I edit, polishing and sharpening over and over. I'm always grateful this works, without really understanding it. Maybe if I understand it, it won't work anymore. Not that I'm superstitious.

All my life, people have told me I shouldn't daydream. I used to get in trouble for it at school. At last I'm absolved. Daydreaming is very useful for writing. I'm lucky my subconscious mind shapes meaning from the sum of my experiences and gives me stories to write. What emerges seems to be a kind of consummate truth, a subterranean home truth. That's why 'What I Didn't Put in My Speech' isn't autobiographical so much as sub-biographical.

I wouldn't describe the writing process as magical. I'd describe it as mysterious and nourishing. I wonder how it is for other people.

REMEMBER

ME

'CARTOGRAPHY'

Tony Birch

There were just the two empty seats on the bus; one behind the driver where a handwritten notice marked TEACHER had been placed, and another down the back, near the exit door. The driver was already warning the kids that they would have to behave themselves. Most were too excited to keep either still or quiet. They were jumping up and down on the seats and calling out to each other across the aisle. They ignored their parents standing on the footpath until the bus pulled away from the kerb, when they broke into a cheer, stamped their feet and waved back excitedly.

We were not yet out of the street before a group of girls, who had earlier commandeered the back seat, began belting out the first lines of a familiar pop song. They had an extensive repertoire and didn't let up until we arrived at our destination a little over a half-hour later.

A week or so earlier my nine-year-old daughter, Meg, had asked me if I would like to accompany her class on their excursion to the new state museum. I wasn't keen on the idea when she surprised me with it over the tea table but hadn't been quick enough with an excuse that might have got me off the hook.

I had been given the lofty title of 'Parent Helper' for the day. When I joined in the line to get onto the bus, Meg's Year Four teacher, Miss Cantrell, presented me with a nametag confirming my status. I was about to slip the tag into my back pocket when she chastised me. 'No, no. You have to actually wear it, displayed in a prominent position. We don't want anyone mistaking you for some creep trying to kidnap one of the kids.'

Even after I had sheepishly pinned the nametag to my shirtfront she gave me that look teachers can't help but give you when you have misbehaved, regardless of your age. I felt like one of the kids from her class who had been caught out doing something wrong. I just did not know what it was.

She wasn't finished with me. 'I see you don't have a plastic bag with you, for your lunch?' she commented.

A boy ahead of me in the line turned around. He was smiling and seemed joyously happy in the knowledge that it was a parent who was in trouble for a change.

'No. I don't have a plastic bag,' I answered her. 'Should I have one?'

'Your lunch then? Where's your lunch?'

'Well … I don't have my lunch with me. I was going to buy something to eat when we get there.'

She was about to chastise me a second time before pursing her lips and saying nothing more, possibly reminding herself that I was actually an independent adult. She chose to roll her eyes sarcastically instead and waved me on to the bus.

The empty seat was alongside a boy, who I had seen a few times before, walking home from school on his own. He was the only child who had not joined in the raucous celebrations when the bus took off. He glanced across at me before returning to the book and pencil case nursed on his lap. He unzipped the case, rifled through it, and brought out a red pencil. He went straight to work, colouring in the letters of a name scrawled across the front cover of the book in the design of a graffiti tag – MORGAN.

I watched as he concentrated on his work, skilfully ensuring that he did not draw outside the lines. After he had coloured in the letters of his name he returned the pencil to the case before looking across at me again. 'Who are you?' he asked, rubbing the tip of his nose with the knuckle of a finger.

'I'm Meg's dad. You know Meg?'

We both looked around to where Meg was sitting, just two rows behind us. Not surprisingly she was with her closest friend, Alice. They had been inseparable from their first day of primary school together.

The boy again rubbed the end of his nose, this time with his palm. 'Yeah, I know Meg. And I know you are her father. But what is your name?'

'My name? Oh, I'm Tom.' I pointed to the cover of his book. 'And you're Morgan?'

He picked up the book and hugged it to his chest as he answered me. 'Yeah, Morgan.'

'Is that a colouring book?' I said.

He appeared mildly insulted by my suggestion. 'No. Colouring books are for kids. Small kids like my baby sister, Angeline. This is a book of maps.'

'Maps? Can I have a look at them?'

He looked me in the face. As he was assessing my character the bus screeched to a halt. Then the driver slammed his hand down on the horn and left it there. Morgan and I, and most everyone on the bus, looked out of the window to see what had happened. We had stopped in heavy traffic outside one the city's largest hospitals. The area in front of the hospital's emergency entrance was crowded with cigarette smokers, all huddled around an ashtray about the size of a forty-four gallon drum.

The majority of the smokers were patients wearing blue hospital gowns or pyjamas, or both. Two men in wheelchairs chatted to each other in between puffing furiously at their cigarettes, while one elderly patient, supporting an IV pole slow-dripping glucose into his veins, attempted to roll himself a smoke. He had the cigarette papers balanced in one hand and a tobacco pouch in the other.

As the bus shunted forward, no more than a few feet at a time, Morgan tapped me on the shoulder. 'Do you want to see my maps?'

Without waiting for a response from me he rested the book in his lap and opened it to the first page, to an elaborately designed border that framed a picture of a large garden. A redbrick building had been drawn in the centre of the garden. The building had a bell tower on the top. It looked very similar to our school building. There was also a large tree in the front garden, just like the ghost gum in our schoolyard.

A series of red arrows led away from the school gate. Morgan had drawn several children into the picture. They were walking home from the school. The arrows travelled around the corner, crossed a road and stopped at the front gate of a wooden house. The house had been coloured-in bright green, while the high-pitched roof was nearly as blue as the sky above it. A sign in the front garden of the house announced that it was HOME.

The smiling face of a child looked out of the front window of the house and across the street, to where two children were standing on the footpath holding hands. I pointed to the face in the window. 'Who is this?'

Morgan tapped on the window. 'That's me. I am in the room I share with my older brother, Nelson.'

I looked across the road to where the couple were standing. 'And these two? Who are they?'

Morgan slapped a hand over his mouth as he tried to stop himself from laughing aloud.

'What is it, Morgan? What's funny?' I asked.

He took his hand away from his mouth, cupped his hands together, leant across the seat and whispered to me. 'I saw from the window, my brother, Nelson. Here.' He pointed to the couple. 'I saw him kiss his girlfriend here, after school. My mother was away at work. They kissed two times.'

He stuck most of his fist in his mouth as he began laughing again.

When he finally stopped laughing he turned the page to a second drawing. It was another map, and used the same colourful border design. I immediately recognised the picture. It was a detailed study of my own suburb. The major roads had been included, as had the playgrounds, the railway stations, the public library and the swimming pool. A series of arrows criss-crossed the map, linking the playgrounds to each other. The streets were full of people, some walking their dogs, kids kicking a football in a park, and families out strolling together.

A KAPOW! cartoon balloon had been drawn near a swing set at one of the playgrounds. I pointed to it. 'What does this mean, Morgan?'

He hesitated before answering me. 'This is where another boy, a bigger boy than me, he punched me.' He made a fist and pushed it into his cheek. 'Here. He hit me here.'

I looked back to the map, to the scene of the crime. I could see a boy standing behind a tree in the park. He appeared to be hiding. I pointed to the boy. 'Is this you, Morgan?'

'No. That's the boy who punched me. I have left him in the park until I can come back with my brother.'

The choirgirls along the back seat interrupted our conversation, by breaking into a chant of 'No! no! no! – we want to go – no! no! no!' as the bus was again forced to a halt in the traffic.

Morgan turned the page to the next drawing. It was a map of greater Melbourne and closely resembled a Melway map. Morgan had attached a foldout section to the book. It allowed him to include the suburbs of the outer west and north, across the city to the beach suburbs and distant hills of the east. Another red arrow journey began at Morgan's house and travelled out along the nearby freeway to the airport, which was marked with drawings of several aircraft.

A second journey headed in the opposite direction and wound its way through the city and onto a highway before heading east.

Morgan nodded in the direction of the airport. 'This is where we arrived in Australia. We landed here in the airplane. When I was smaller.'

He followed the second set of arrows from his house. Morgan crossed busy intersections, he travelled over bridges and along empty highways, until he arrived at a spot on the map where a thick black cross had been drawn, marking the end of his destination.

'And this is where my other family live. My cousins and aunties and uncles, they all live here.' He then retraced his steps back to his own house. 'I don't see my cousins anymore. It's a long way to go.'

He quickly turned the page to the next drawing. It was a map of Australia, coloured in various shades of green around the edges and browns and dull yellows across the centre. Each of the states and territories had been mapped and named, as had the capital cities and some natural features, including mountain ranges and rivers. I could see an aircraft flying to the right of ULURU – BIGGEST ROCK IN THE WORLD!

I looked towards the Indian Ocean, located on one edge of the map and coloured a deep green. 'Where are you from, Morgan?'

He answered by turning the page to yet another map, showing the continent of Africa. Each country had been named and shaded in soft colours. Another aeroplane was about to land on a narrow strip of land on the east coast. Morgan touched the aircraft lightly. 'We are from here. My family come from Somalia.'

I could hear a siren approaching us from behind. When an ambulance sped by the bus the children screamed with a mix of excitement and apprehension. The bus driver grabbed a microphone from the dashboard as the bus stopped again. 'Okay, kids. Take it easy. We've got a problem up ahead. We'll just have to sit tight for a few minutes.'

Morgan turned the page to the final drawing in the book. It was another large city. The streets were crowded with buses and bicycles and people, and dogs, lots of dogs.

I ran a hand over the map. 'There's so much information here, Morgan. You must have a good memory for places?'

He shook his head vigorously. 'No. I don't remember anything about Africa. I was too young when we came. I made this drawing from books with pictures of my country. And stories. Stories from my mother and from my family.'

I followed Morgan's final journey from the airport. It ended abruptly on the far side of the city at a location also marked with a heavy cross. 'And this is where you lived when you were younger?' I asked him, pointing to the cross.

Morgan said nothing as he slowly closed the book. He picked up a plastic bag from under his seat. It contained his lunch. He put the book in the bag and returned it to the floor. Then he leant his head against the window and closed his eyes.

When we finally took off again every kid on the bus, from the front seats to the back, broke into spontaneous applause. They quietened almost as quickly when the ambulance sped by a second time with its siren blaring. It was heading in the direction we had just come from.

I realised what had caused our delay when we passed a car wreck in the middle of the next intersection. The roof of the car had been torn open like a can of beans, and the passenger side doors had been crushed in. A tow-truck driver in overalls was sweeping shattered glass from the road, while a fire-fighter hosed down the gutter. A stream of water laced with patterns of dark oil ran towards the drain.

Most of the children moved to one side of the bus and looked out through the window at the accident until Miss Cantrell stood up and loudly clapped her hands together several times. 'Children. Back to your seats.'

Morgan tapped me on the arm. 'The cross in my picture, it's not of my home. We came from our village to the city, so that we could leave for another place.' He covered the cross with the tip of his finger. 'This is the graveyard.' Morgan looked at me calmly as his chest quietly rose with each breath.

The girls along the back seat broke into another rhythmic clap and chant as soon as they spotted the giant Rubik's Cube out front of the museum.

When the bus pulled into the kerb Miss Cantrell got to her feet. 'Okay. Everybody. Now listen. We will get off the bus in pairs. And we will remain in pairs. Hold hands with your partner. And please stay together.'

Meg and Alice stood up. They took each other by the hand, skipped down the aisle, and jumped off the bus.

With the exception of the driver, who was waiting in the doorway for everyone to leave, I was the final passenger to get off the bus. Morgan was waiting for me on the footpath.

A HAND OF FRIENDSHIP: WRITING 'CARTOGRAPHY'

essay by Tony Birch

I have been writing and publishing fiction for fifteen years. My first book, *Shadowboxing*, is set around inner Melbourne, in the suburbs of Fitzroy, Richmond, Collingwood and Carlton. My second book, *Father's Day*, explored similar physical and psychological geographies and place, and I have since focused strongly on Melbourne's Yarra River as the site of much of my fiction. I now live only a couple of hundred metres from the house I was born in, and spend a great deal of my spare time walking streets of such familiarity. It is unlikely that there is a street in either Carlton or Fitzroy that I have not walked down, and knowing *my place* so accurately provides me with a high degree of emotional security.

The idea for 'Cartography' came to me while accompanying my youngest daughter, Nina, on a school excursion to the Melbourne Museum in the Carlton Gardens. Similar to the fictional story, while on the bus I discreetly observed my daughter amongst her friends. I was pleasantly struck by how happy she seemed, totally at ease with her friends and her circumstances. It may not appear to be a great revelation, but it is, for a parent who may be anxious about a child's general wellbeing. I could not say that other children on the bus were unhappy, but as would be expected within a

Year Five class, other kids appeared more reserved, social observers rather than participants.

This is several years ago now. It was a time when a number of children from Somalia had enrolled at the school after coming to Australia as refugees with their families, fleeing strife in their home country. These kids were accepted quickly into a school community that has historically been genuinely diverse, having educated a high proportion of migrant kids, mostly Greek and Italian in the 1950s and 1960s, and children from the Middle East in the 1970s. And yet, on that bus trip that morning I noticed that a couple of the Somalian children were sitting alone.

The child I sat next to was one of those kids. His name was not Morgan, and he did not have a book of maps in his lap. But he carried a remarkable knowledge of the streets of Melbourne in his head. I had introduced myself to him and sat down. As the bus took off I noticed that he was watching me closely. Being an experienced parent of five children I suspected there was something he wanted to say to me. I broke the ice by chatting about something I can no longer remember. As also happens in the story, the bus quickly got stuck in traffic. The boy turned to me and asked the question, 'Do you know how to get to the MCG?' I thought it was an odd question, and that maybe he thought the school excursion was heading to the Cricket Ground and not the Museum.

I eventually answered his question, providing the vaguest of directions. He then said, 'I know another way,' and proceeded to name each street and every turn you would need to take from where we were stuck in traffic to the ground. He continued to ask similar questions of me, such as, 'How would you go to the airport?' and 'Which roads would you take from here to Dandenong?' (It turned out that the boy had extended family living in Dandenong that he regularly visited.) Again, he was able to recite in great detail the route he needed to take to arrive at his destinations safely and on time.

The boy was a human GPS system. His ability reminded me of the test applied to prospective London cabbies, whose knowledge of how to get from one destination to another is tested before they are granted a licence. But why a ten-year-old boy would memorise the streets of Melbourne intrigued me. So I asked him. His answer, as simple as it was, left me with a lot to think about. He told me that soon after his arrival in Melbourne, and the family's move into the same suburb I lived in, he was out on his own one day when he became lost. He walked the streets for several hours and eventually found his way home in the dark, and in the rain.

'I did not want to be lost again,' he told me. 'So, I found a book of maps of the city in the Salvation Army shop. I read them every night and test myself. I do not want to be lost again.'

I thought about the boy that night as I was watching my daughter across the kitchen table, talking excitedly about her visit to the museum. Like me, she is a keen walker, knows her streets well, and could then, and now, easily find her way home. This, we take for granted. Those who come here from other parts of the world have to learn and experience their knowledge of place. My young friend on the bus that morning taught me a lesson. Not only did I take my own sense of security of place for granted, I lacked knowledge of the extent of anxiety that a person who has been displaced may experience.

*

When it came to writing 'Cartography' I had initial concepts in mind. I wanted to juxtapose the narrator's observation of his daughter's contentment with the experiences of the boy, Morgan, who could not take his place for granted. What I did not want to do was alienate the character from either his classmates or his surroundings. Like Morgan, the boy that I sat next to was not ostracised from his classmates (I have seen him front and centre in the school playground both before and after the excursion). Nor was he alienated from *place*. What he had done was discover a means with which he could provide a sense of security for himself until experience and familiarity took over.

I also did not want to tell the story through the actual conversation I had with the boy. I have long had an interest in reading maps, and as a young boy I also sought out old street directories in secondhand shops, took them home and re-drew them with colouring pencils, adding details. While I did know the streets of my childhood quite well, like Morgan, I added landscapes to the street maps that reproduced a narrative of my particular experience. In the case of Morgan, and in writing the first drafts of the story, I never felt that I could 'get inside his head', and imagine what a boy like Morgan might be thinking. I do not have the refugee experience that might provide that. I stuck to my intuition about children in general, and when thinking about place, considered what might sadden them, what situations would worry them, and experiences of place that would create happiness (such as the drawing of Morgan watching his brother kiss a girl outside his window).

I imagined Morgan's book of maps functioning as a traditional child's storybook, and that as each page is turned we move from the immediate and local to the story of the journey that begins on the other side of the world. Through this simple storyboard approach I hoped to provide the simplest of understandings as to what the migrant journey is about. I regard 'simplicity' in this case as appropriate to the story in two keys ways. First, that it fits the format of the story produced by Morgan, a storybook. And second, I wanted to write a story that, while written for any age group, would speak to children such as those on the bus that morning.

Another conceptual imperative driving the writing of 'Cartography' was that I wanted to illustrate the generosity in Morgan – his decision to share his book of maps and his journey with his adult companion, a man he hardly knows. While he is initially a little hesitant to engage with the narrator, Morgan is also eager to tell his story. I regard this as a strong ethical foundation to storytelling, that we listen to, and respect, the stories of others. The outcome enriches both storyteller and audience. Thinking about refugees that have arrived in Australia in the last two decades, there are communities that are often spoken about and for, but are provided with limited opportunity to tell their own story. We need to provide a space for these stories to be told and heard.

I thought a great deal about the ending of the story. As with Meg and Alice in the fictional story on the bus that morning, I watched as Nina skipped off the bus with one of her closest friends. The affection between them was obvious. I thought about the possibility of Tom offering his hand of friendship to Morgan. Initially, this approach seemed obvious – the hand of the *host* offering *sanctuary* to the outsider. But it troubled me. It was too easy, and more than a little patronising. I then had an image of Morgan, standing outside the bus, alone on the footpath. This could have been a lonely, and again, alienating image. I did not want to end the story this way, and I do not think it matched its overall tone. I remember sleeping on my creative dilemma, unsure of what to do.

The idea that Morgan waits for Tom was satisfying. I didn't want an ending that was either melodramatic or sentimental. But I did want the characters to emotionally connect with each other and the reader. Morgan and Tom become equals in some sense. They are both apprehensive. And yet they have chosen, perhaps unconsciously, but as a result of this brief encounter, to turn to each other.

I have written many stories over the years. 'Cartography' is one of my more satisfying works as I feel the story does what I hoped it would do. In a subtle and quiet way I feel that it does ask readers to contemplate the experience of the *outsider* through the eyes of a child, a creatively minded boy, Morgan, who is both innocent and experienced to a degree that many of us do not reach in a lifetime. I believe there are many Morgans out there. They have many stories to tell us. When they offer them I hope that we have the understanding to turn to them and receive their stories with generous hearts.

'MY ABBR.D LIFE'

Michael Giacometti

My ma is a self-mutilating alcoholic. She was beautiful, Nanna says with a hint of a smile shaking her head, but wilful. I see it. Her slender emu legs, her sexy doggy dance, her don't-mess-with-me glare. Might be all you see is red hate-filled eyes, the stink of vomit and sweat and piss and meat embedded in her hair and skin, the ripped and stained dress, the obvious sorry scars, the soiled bandages on her head and forearm and foot. You see a wasted life in need of redemption ... or another rock to the head; I see my ma.

But I don't see her much. Nanna grows me up. Like in old times, she says, the old ones stay in camp and teach the young ones while the women go out and gather food for them all. Only difference is Ma gathers nothing for us, no matter how much Nanna and Auntie harass her like willy-wagtails at a crow, she spends her whole time playing cards with the weekly handout for the big kitty or following the green-can-dreaming along the sandy river bed.

Nanna says Ma wants to drown her sorrows because her ma was stolen from her, but Ma isn't sinking, all that grog is keeping her afloat. Even when uncle lies on her she doesn't go under. Thinking he is a stone she clings to him, but must be he is full of air and she floats. Even his fists are puffy clouds. Her skin absorbs all they rain down on her.

Ma is swimming in that river of grog when I jump into her belly. My milk is 90 proof. I emerge from her cave like a joey: undersized, soft and squishy right through. No words form on my tongue. I keep crawling when other kids are kicking the footy and taking hangers.

Uncle take me many times. I am promised to him at birth. But he take me, he take me from Auntie's breast. He smell of booze and ganja and mulga smoke. The uncles play a dvd showing naked people doing grunting things. Cousins sit on the floor in front of the tv like the best kids in class. Uncle laughs. He calls me marsupial mole. He says, I speared me little mole. The uncles laugh too. Their spears are hard and sharp; they move with purpose.

When Ma is sober she sometimes brings hot chips with gravy and cool drinks from the community shop. My gums bleed. When Ma leaves I cling to her. She growls at me and punches her love into bruises that flower darker than my skin. I try to make them last until Ma touches me again.

I don't resist when my sister cuts a Coke can in half, pierces a couple of holes in the jagged rim and puts a piece of wire through. She hangs it over my head like a feed bag and pours in a little purple liquid from a plastic bottle. Don't drink it, she signs with a hand and nose, sniff. Like them mob there, she points, the skinny, shuffling, mumbling ghost kids with bulging eyes. It is sweet oblivion. I am … finally … close to Ma.

The notices in the paper call me no name, out of cultural respect, or shame. Iloveyousoverymuchmychild, Ma slurs and cuts her bare breast deep and bleeds into dust. Aunties plastered in white clay drone wetly and pull out their hair. They do it for me.

My name is Shantitia Hames. I was six years old.

THE MADNESS OR THE METHOD

essay by Michael Giacometti

The first sentence is an act of strong magic. It is the seductive desire that lures you, the reader, lures you in like a crow to fresh roadkill. It is the director shouting 'Action' and action starts now. It is a boxer putting you on your arse with the first punch. (Raymond Carver via Paddy O'Reilly and Mary Manning taught me that.) It is the gelatine that sets the tone, perspective and voice. It tells you something important. It should intrigue. But mostly, it must unsettle. It is a cattleprod, a hard slap.

My ma is a self-mutilating alcoholic.

Jolt.

But before reading the first line, the story title has frontloaded some level of expectation. There is no way a completed story, let alone one in progress, could be left untitled. The title must inspire me and spur me to write. I choose it deliberately. It rarely changes. It is an invitation for you to read further. It may be all the potential reader reads. It is a chance for poetry.

My (first person) *abbr.d* (consciously odd abbreviation, probably of the word 'abbreviated') *life.*

My odd cut-short life.

*

Story development often begins with a title and a single idea or image or brief scene. The story is eventually constructed around that core, but it undergoes a long gestation before it is sufficiently developed. Like a kangaroo I am pregnant-in-permanence with story. They are like embryonic kangaroos, remaining in diapause, a state of frozen development, until there is plentiful feed or the sibling joey is able to leave the pouch. For me the landscape is mainly droughty. My output is limited in quantity and terribly slow in development.

I thought it would be an easy gig to comment on the method and inspiration for one of my stories. After all, I call myself a writer. But I have struggled for months to unearth and describe it. What is my method? It is a self-exposing question.

During meditations I mentally composed more than five different expositions. For each I thought, yes, this is how. But each one told only part of the story. I couldn't decide which to use. I committed none of them to paper. Now I can't remember any of them. This is what you get instead.

What is your method for writing stories? It sounded like a trap. The deadline after the deadline had passed. Send us what you have, the editors pleaded. It's very rough, I replied. Send it anyway, they urged.

What I sent was a mass of disjointed blocks of text related to the theme, often repetitive, written over months. The blocks sat on the page in the time sequence they were written, not yet ordered into common themes. They began as random ideas and notes, possibly scribbled on a napkin or shred of scrap and placed in a pile of similar scraps, then typed up as a jigsaw piece at a later date. I sent what I blinkered myself from, what I dared not admit, what I feared would expose me as a charlatan writer. A Brahmin palm-reader on an Indian train once told me that I didn't have the hands of a writer. I feared revealing that truth.

I sent, I finally shockingly realised, my 'method' in progress. The 'rough' is my method.

My mentor, Melanie Ostell, recently observed that I write for the line, for the words and the sounds, and not for the overall structure. Structure comes later. She could see that by reading just one story of mine. From the initial core idea or vision I imagine an elusive jigsaw box cover. The disjointed chunks of text are the inadequate pieces of the jigsaw. Pieces are moved around. Reshaped. Some slot together seamlessly. Some create new pieces at will. Some pieces jar with others like musicians slightly off key. To admit this is to admit not being perfect. To admit this is to admit my own fallibility.

So what is my method? This essay is a metaphor for my writing method.

But the genesis of 'my abbr.d life' was atypical.

It was conceived during a summer dog walk in the hills around Alice Springs as a homage to my long-deceased father. The idea: to write a post-postmodernist story composed entirely of truncated and abbreviated text to be deciphered by the reader, thus inviting many interpretations. I had a title. I wrote two brief alternative paragraphs. But they were stillborn.

The next day, on somewhat the same walk, the title still swimming in my mind with the intent of semen to spear the egg, and a young Aboriginal girl who was born with foetal alcohol syndrome to a gambling alcoholic mother, a girl who was repeatedly molested by the men, who died from the outback scourge petrol sniffing, who for Aboriginal cultural reasons should remain nameless so her spirit can be at rest but who for reasons of shame I gave her the name Shantitia Hames, it was she that leapt out of the earth to be reborn in me and out from me. I returned home, sat down, wrote the story complete in one sitting.

*

I recall when Arnold Zable stayed for a few nights. He had filled his last journal and fretted about finding a replacement in town. His daily need to dictate thoughts and experiences and ideas and observations was an addiction that I do not share. I endeavour to carry a notepad and pen with me most of the time, especially when out walking, but often forget. Yet even when I remember, I rarely write in it. I do not keep a daily journal, not even when travelling. If I am not a writer, what am I? I am an observer that sometimes writes.

I store observations in the cupboards of my mind. Events and people and inanimate things, feelings and senses and opinions. They are eclectic and poorly catalogued.

Nine years ago when I first came to Central Australia to live and work I thought I knew a bit about Indigenous people. What I had read could not prepare me for what I then saw and heard and smelt and felt. I knew less than nothing. I read widely from anthropologists like Stanner, explorers' journals, Indigenous oral histories, and Indigenous cultural knowledge – language, medicine, and bushtucker. I worked for Indigenous organisations, played football, had Indigenous neighbours that became like extended family, was 'adopted' by a 'wife' and given a skin name, my wife and dog also, so that I was defined within the cultural rights and responsibilities and protocols of the Indigenous community.

I knew less than nothing. Now, after learning some, I realise how much more there is to know that will never be revealed. I knew one hundred per cent of nothing. Now I know less than one per cent of something. And the longer I live here in Central Australia the more the black and white opinions mix into a murky grey.

In October 2010, a senior traditional custodian for Alice Springs conducted a tour of local sacred sites for local artists and writers. She talked about the meaning of those places, of how the past overlays the present and vice versa into an 'everywhen', of a continual struggle with authorities to maintain the integrity of the places. And she encouraged us to explore in our art the grey zone, the boundary of inter-cultural tension, to further inform some kind of understanding by whitefellas in Alice Springs and the big cities. The conscious mind makes journals. The unconscious mind exhumes profound writing. It was from this deep spring in the eroded granite hills that Shantitia Hames seeped.

Hames. An anagram of 'shame'. And with her, her mother and an ever-present extended family group of cousins and aunties and uncles. Not focusing on a single incident or moment, but describing an agglomeration of incidents, a history of the oppressed. With a language informed by the vernacular of Indigenous desert people: not chicken legs but emu legs (long and very lean, fast running), cool drinks (because they can't remain icy in 40 degree heat) instead of cold drinks.

*

Shantitia Hames and her extended family are entirely fictional. They are not based on any actual person, living or deceased. The story's plot is my invention. Although the events portrayed have occurred in many Indigenous communities, the fiction does not appropriate anyone's story or lived experience. I am not retelling someone else's story in more eloquent words. I know of no person living or that has lived named Shantitia Hames. If there is someone by that name then I humbly apologise to her and her family for any sorrow caused. The story is entirely a work of my invention.

I am an educated middle-class whitefella approaching middle age. Writing fiction allows me to inhabit a diversity of characters that are not me. A hangman, a Latino couple, an impaled railway signalman, a snail, a Tibetan monk, a pregnant woman. No problems. But a dead Aboriginal girl? Eyebrows raise and mouths open. Will some kind of fatwa or curse be cast upon me? A sickness of stones and bones in my gut and incurable headaches. A wind that blows only me off balance. This is my ongoing dilemma.

In a discussion paper about the representation of Indigenous people and culture in Australian literature, Dr Anita Heiss states:

> Some Indigenous people question whether non-Indigenous people should write about Indigenous people at all, be it Indigenous history or the portrayal of an Indigenous character … [due to] … the history of negative

> representation of Aboriginal and Torres Strait Islanders that has proliferated in the writing world.[1]

The Literature Board of the Australia Council for the Arts subsequently developed protocols for producing Indigenous Australian writing. The protocols suggest four key questions for writing about Indigenous people and culture:

> How will your writing affect the Indigenous group it is based on?
>
> Does it empower them?
>
> Does it expose confidential or personal and sensitive material?
>
> Does it reinforce negative stereotypes?[2]

And to these I add two of my own construction:

> Does it deserve to be told in the public domain?
>
> Do you have the right to tell it?

'My abbr.d life' was not based on any particular Indigenous language group or people. There is nothing in the story that suggests it was. I never intended to target or stigmatise Indigenous people, rather the lack of identification makes the story more universal. Often the word 'empower' is misconstrued. A negative ideal can be given authority just as much as a positive one. This story is like the *Little Children are Sacred Report*[3] that highlighted widespread sexual abuse in Indigenous communities and sparked a heavy-handed government intervention. It states what is happening. By doing so maybe some people, the women, the men, will stand up and take action themselves within community.

There is no sacred or taboo information revealed in 'my abbr.d life' that should be withheld from women, children or the uninitiated. It is not a record of oral history. There is shame in stating the deceased's name. Excising her name from speech so that her spirit does not attach itself to her living place and things is part of grief and healing. But she demands, by naming herself, that her shame must not be repeated.

Some negative stereotypes may be reinforced, of drunks, domestic violence, sexual abuse, drug use, hopelessness and apathy. Warwick Thornton's film *Samson and Delilah* premiered at the 2009 Adelaide Film Festival. A friend who attended sat beside a Kaurna elder. As the film progressed and the tragedy unfolded, the elder grew increasingly agitated. At the end, while the rest of the audience stood and applauded in appreciation, she remained seated, her hands squeezed between her thighs, indignant that her people, Indigenous people, were represented in such a hopeless negative way. But Thornton is an Indigenous man from Alice Springs. Surely he has the right to comment on his own people, highlight what is happening, and show a glimmer of redemption. Because if he can't, who can?

*

The events described in 'my abbr.d life' have occurred and do occur in Indigenous communities despite the best intentions and efforts of many blackfella and whitefella organisations and individuals. Living here is like being in a foreign developing country with a large ex-pat community. It is Australia, yes, but the land (and so too the people) are Arrernte, Warlpiri, Luritja, Pitjantjatjara, Anmatjere and more. The inter-cultural collide is the point of tension in the landscape. To live and work here, this tension needs to be reconciled in some way. Otherwise people burn out rapidly. Some sing, play sport. Some form death metal bands, others drink excessively. Everyone gossips. Writing helps me to make some sense of the complexities and contradictions of this place.

I constantly wrestle with the question of whether I should write from an Indigenous person's perspective. It is my opinion and observation, not theirs. Can I inhabit a world that is culturally opposite to mine? I am reticent to read my Indigenous writing in Alice Springs, fearing what people might think, how they will judge me. Like telling secrets to a stranger, I am comfortable reading them elsewhere.

The Indigenous story, as Janke states, '… has encoded messages of law, land, place, knowledge, experience and survival. It is the underlying script for Indigenous cultural identity'.[4]

I could say that I didn't write this story, that the land gave it to me complete, but that might be pushing the whitefella connection with the spiritual landscape into even more dangerous territory. I have tried to view my inspiration *post scriptum* objectively. There are many culturally insensitive stories and books in the public domain. I pray that I have not contributed another.

Endnotes

1. Heiss, A. *Writing about Indigenous Australia: some issues to consider and protocols to follow – a discussion paper*, Australian Society of Authors, 2002, http://www.asauthors.org/asa-papers/writing-about-Indigenuos-australia.pdf, accessed 5 September 2013.

2. Janke, T. *More than words: writing, Indigenous culture & copyright in Australia*, Australian Society of Authors, 2009, http://www.asauthors.org/files/pages/writing_about_indigenous_australia.pdf, accessed 5 September 2013.

3. Northern Territory Board of Inquiry into the Protection of Aboriginal Children from Sexual Abuse, *Ampe Akelyernemane Meke Mekarle 'Little Children are Sacred'*, Northern Territory Government, 2007, http://www.lowitja.org.au/little-children-are-sacred, accessed 17 February 2014.

4. Janke, T. *Writing Protocols for producing Indigenous Australian writing*, 2nd edn., Australia Council for the Arts, 2007, http://www.australiacouncil.gov.au/resources/reports_and_publications/artforms/literature/writing_protocols_for_producing_indigenous_australian_writing.pdf, accessed 31 October 2013.

'GOOD RUBBISH'

Andy Kissane

Ratha was standing in garbage that came up to his knees. In his right hand he held his hook – a straight iron rod a metre long that curved at the end into a very sharp point. When Ratha put the handle on the ground the point was level with his eyes. It was a useful tool, one that he wielded skilfully as he sifted through the rubbish.

In his left hand he held a hessian sack that he was filling with plastic bags. When he spotted a bag, he pierced it with his hook, extended his arm while he shook the filth from the bag, then dropped it into his sack. A process he performed in a few seconds, as quickly and as easily as he stopped a football with his chest, steadied it with his left foot and dispatched it with his right. He played football every afternoon and spent much of the day dreaming of his first goal, how it would glide off his toes and cannon into the net.

The flies rose as Ratha worked, a flotilla of black and green scavengers that were never short of sustenance. Flies that were probably born in the Stung Meanchey dump in Phnom Penh and would no doubt spend their luxurious lives there, squirming and burrowing into acres of putrid, decaying waste. Mostly the flies didn't bother Ratha, except when they came in packs to land on his eyes, his lips, his ears. He had taken to wearing a scarf pulled up high over his nose and tied around his head, like a cowboy in a western, as well as a cap, the peak hiding his eyebrows. The more skin he left exposed, the more trouble he had with flies.

Ratha knew a lot about rubbish. How it tended to stick together, glued into place by food scraps – by prawn shells, ropey egg noodles and the black seedy pulp of pawpaws. How the bags filled with bones from the butcher's or the overripe fruit from the markets attracted the most flies. How it was rare to find anything that was fresh enough to eat. How people only threw away food that looked diseased – the bloated carcass of a spatchcock crawling with maggots or the innards of fish putrefying in the sun and giving off a smell you wanted to run away from. How plastic could be reused to manufacture paint, while a full sack of metal earned you the most riels. How chemical waste had the worst smell of all and how it was better to avoid the trucks that dumped chemicals because they made your eyes water and covered your skin with rashes. And how no one had a better understanding of the cargoes of trucks and the daily workings of Stung Meanchey than his friend, Thavery. She was the cleverest and fastest girl on the dump, a girl who regularly made five thousand riels a day.

A hook suddenly jolted against his hook and Ratha did not even turn around. He knew that Thavery was standing there, beaming. She loved sneaking up on him.

'Found anything?' she asked.

'Just plastic today.'

'There's good rubbish near the main road. Let's go.'

Ratha picked up his sack and followed Thavery, carefully stepping into her footsteps so as to not sink down into some hidden hole. They weaved through the garbage until they reached the dirt track.

Thavery stopped while she pulled her red checked scarf over her head, then raced off, her hook leading the way. Ratha was right behind her. If you were slow, Thavery would use her hook to flick a pellet of mud at you, or an orange skin or some other noxious tidbit, often firing over her shoulder without even looking. She had an uncanny ability to hit you exactly when you weren't expecting it. She was a menace with that hook. The boys sometimes teased Ratha for foraging with Thavery, but he still met her most afternoons on her way home from school. She usually knew where she wanted to go. 'Along the road that leads to the sick lake will be good for us,' she'd say or 'Truck twenty-three is unloading near the small mountain.' Thavery had worked all her life at the dump; she knew things that Ratha was still learning. She had eyes as keen as an eagle's and when she spotted something she swooped on it.

She strolled towards a mound of rubbish on their left that was scattered with plastic bags. Ratha scooped up a couple of bags and dropped them into his sack. But Thavery ignored the bags and poked about in a jumble of leaves, palm fronds and bamboo sticks. The green waste was generally worthless, so Ratha wondered what Thavery was up to. Suddenly she pushed a pile of leaves away to reveal a birdcage. The door of the cage was missing, but the wire appeared to be rust-free and valuable. Thavery reached into the cage and brought out a camera. It was probably faulty, but even a faulty camera was worth a lot of money.

Thavery held it up and said, 'Smile.'

Ratha stood there grinning, his hook pointing up to the sky, his bag swollen.

Thavery gave Ratha the camera and he pretended to take her photo, her white teeth shining, her checked scarf caught by the wind as if it was about to lift off her head. Then Thavery put the camera into her sack and together they carried the birdcage towards her hut. Her mother would know what to do with the camera, who to sell it to.

Minea was sitting up outside the hut, grinding rice in a stone mill to make noodles. 'Home already?' she asked.

'Look, Mak, look,' Thavery said, letting go of the cage so it nearly fell on Ratha's foot. She rushed forward, taking the camera out of the sack.

'You've found a treasure,' Minea said, examining the camera.

'Is it worth much?'

'We'll find out soon enough.' Minea put the wet, doughy ball into a cloth bag, placed the bag down on a wooden shelf outside the hut and put a rock on top. She told them to leave the birdcage and their hooks inside. They would start straightaway for the street of the repairmen and be back before Ratha was missed. She picked up two bottles of water from a low table and gave one to each child. She tied a yellow scarf over her head and they set off.

The sun was high in the sky, but they couldn't afford a rickshaw. They walked a long way along the road to Phnom Penh. Ratha was excited. It was hot, but there weren't as many flies. A swarm of motorbikes, cyclos, cars and trucks streamed past, heading in both directions. They walked on the stony edge and breathed in the fumes. It was impossible to hear anyone talk above the chorus of horns and the roar of the traffic, but Ratha was glad to leave the dump, even for a few hours.

The street of the repairmen was barely wide enough for a rickshaw. Men stood outside the shops smoking and talking and a crowd seemed to follow the three of them wherever they went. The process was the same in every shop – a man would examine the camera carefully, then declare that the lenses were fine, the shutter mechanism faulty. Although Minea tried to bargain, the most she was offered was thirty thousand riels.

The fourth shop was run by an old man who ushered them to three seats and asked a boy to bring them tea. He worked under the light of a single, dusty globe hanging from the ceiling. His beard was so long it threatened to get caught in the camera. He was so slow, so meticulous that Thavery finished her tea, then wandered around the shop. He saw Thavery staring at a tray of necklaces, stroked his white beard and offered Minea a necklace as well as thirty-two thousand riels for the camera. Minea glanced at her daughter and immediately accepted.

Thavery chose a necklace of shiny silver beads shaped like cone shells, interspersed with smaller blue beads. The beads had lustre, though they weren't really silver.

'It's more stylish than what the other girls wear,' she told Ratha on the way home. Ratha hadn't noticed any of the girls' necklaces, but from that day on he never saw Thavery without hers. Sometimes when they were resting she ran her fingers over the beads; sometimes she polished them with the tail of her shirt.

'I'm so lucky,' she told Ratha, 'especially as Mak says I'll never have to sell it, no matter how poor we are.'

*

When Ratha woke the following morning it was dark and his aunt, Seak, was sleeping. His uncle, Bo, was not beside her. Probably Bo had drunk too much rice wine and gone to sleep on someone else's floor. Seak had told Ratha that he must not grow up into a bad man like Bo, that he must always come home to his wife.

Ratha watched a gecko crawl up the wall above his head. The gecko had a long tail, red spots and eyes like yellow marbles. Ratha was hungry and thought for a moment about catching the gecko. But it was not really fat enough to eat. It wasn't a very smart gecko because there was never much food in the hut. Unless it caught mosquitoes when Ratha wasn't looking and squashed them. Ratha hated mosquitoes, hated the way they hung around like pesky little sisters and did not ask before biting. Seak said it was rude to eat without asking, without giving thanks, but the mosquitoes took no notice of her. They were greedy and often kept him awake during the months of the monsoon.

Sitting up, Ratha slipped his feet into his boots. He had been living here for almost a year, ever since his mother died. His aunt would wake soon and he wanted to leave the hut before she asked him to help with the younger children. He crept past his sister and his three cousins, pushed the flap of the door open and was gone. He smelt the stench as soon as he was outside. When there was no wind, the gases released by the festering, rotting waste had nowhere to go and a cloud of foul air smothered the dump. The mountain was still smoking from yesterday's fires; the sky was beginning to show the first signs of dawn. Ratha turned towards the French school and ran. He was too early for the breakfast they served to the schoolchildren, but he knew a man who worked in the kitchen who would look after him. He ran through the school gates, under the dining tarpaulin, past the long tables and up to the serving bench.

As usual, Emile was standing next to the large saucepans filled with rice. 'Good morning, Ratha.'

'Hello, Emile.'

'Rice?'

'Please.'

'You will stay for school, then?'

Ratha nodded.

'I'll take your boots and give them back when school's over.' This was what Emile always said while he filled a bowl with rice. One day, Emile had bent down as if he was going to grab Ratha's boots and Ratha had sprinted away. Since then they had just joked about school.

Ratha felt the warmth of the rice through the bottom of the bowl. He walked to one of the tables and sat down. The rice was gluggy and soft. He chewed quickly, eating the first few mouthfuls with his fingers. Then, as he saw Emile approaching, he picked up the spoon and used it to scoop up the rice.

Emile put a cup of tea down on the table and took the chair opposite him. 'So Ratha, what will you do today?'

'I'll play football,' Ratha replied. 'And score a goal.'

'Ah, like yesterday?'

'I didn't score yesterday.'

'Too bad.' Emile pushed the cup of tea towards him.

They had had this conversation before. The routine was reassuring.

'If you score, will you take some lessons?' Emile asked.

'Yes.'

But when his stomach was full, he always said yes, he didn't want to disappoint Emile. Anyway, he would probably never score. The other boys were too big and did not pass. They just dribbled the ball as if they were Ronaldo and shot from a long way out. When they scored, they ran around with bare chests, twirling their shirts in the air. Ratha thought it was probably what Ronaldo did when he scored. The boys played on a pitch without goalposts, using their hooks and hessian sacks to mark the position of the goals. So naturally, there were many arguments about goals. Whenever the others argued, Ratha practised dribbling the ball, weaving up and down the pitch until the dispute was finally settled.

'Would you like more?' Emile asked, when Ratha had finished.

Ratha shook his head. 'I'm off to get my schoolbooks.'

Emile laughed and shook Ratha's hand, bending over so his face was close to the boy's. 'Very good, Ratha. And make sure you don't tell my boss about breakfast.'

Ratha lifted his finger to his lips and made a sound he had learnt from Emile, the sound of the wind gusting. Because Emile let him eat before the other children, Ratha was one of the first to start work. The earlier he began the more time he had for football. He set off for the hut to collect his hook and sack. The sky was now a dirty mottled pink, like the skin of a fish.

He wanted to find football boots like the single Adidas boot with the missing studs that Kayrith wore. Kayrith ran funny with only one boot on, but it still made him the undisputed captain of the Red Devils. Most of all, Ratha wanted to find a Red Devils shirt, for with a shirt like that he would be able to lead the Devils and the boys would want to pass him the ball. But why would anyone throw away something so precious?

*

On a Sunday, when there was no school, Ratha followed Thavery along the road that wound around the perimeter of Stung

Meanchey. In some places, the rubbish was so sparse you could actually see the earth beneath each step.

Suddenly Thavery cried out, raced up a slight rise, knelt down and began digging.

When Ratha reached her, he saw two plastic legs sticking out of the ground. Thavery soon had the dirt loose enough and she lifted up a thin, naked doll with a skinny torso and very long legs. The doll had straight blond hair that almost reached down to her waist. Thavery brushed the dirt away. She turned the doll over and over. It had two arms and two legs and did not appear to be broken. She grinned at Ratha.

'Will you sell it?'

'Maybe. I'll wash the mud off and plait her hair. Then make some clothes. These dolls have clothes.'

'How do you know?'

'I've seen them in magazines. They're called Barbie.'

'This doll is called Barbie?'

'All these dolls are called Barbie.'

Ratha wondered why anyone would give two dolls the same name. 'How many Barbies are there?'

'Many, many Barbies. Now I have one too.'

Perhaps Thavery had learnt this at school, Ratha thought.

'Don't tell anyone about the doll.'

'I won't.'

'I must go.' Thavery ran off, holding the doll up so her hair streamed back like the tail of a kite. She sprinted towards the creek where the women did their washing.

Ratha started to follow her, then changed his mind. The huts were in the opposite direction and he was hungry. Maybe his aunt had something to eat, anything at all, for his stomach ached, his head was sore, and here was this dizziness again that made it so hard to walk along the track.

*

A few weeks later, when the two friends were working high up on the mountain, they came across a load of plastic bottles that had been missed. Thavery was particularly pleased whenever the bottles had tops. 'Keep the tops,' she told Ratha. 'We can use them.'

Ratha wasn't sure why the tops were important, but he followed Thavery's advice. Their sacks filled quickly and they set off for the main road that led to the manager's hut. But instead of turning left at the road, Thavery insisted on turning right.

Ratha was tempted to hide his sack and return for it later, but he'd lose thousands of riels if anyone found it and took it to the weighing station.

'Why do you go to school, when you could be working?' Ratha asked, brushing a fly off his nose.

'I don't want to stay here. I want to work as a hairdresser. Or a beautician.'

'You get paid for that?'

'Sure. People pay to have their hair cut and styled, they pay to have their fingernails painted, they pay to have their faces packed in mud, their skins cleansed.'

Ratha laughed. 'Plenty of free mud around here.'

Thavery laughed too. 'It's not that sort of mud.'

They had left the road and were now walking towards the sick lake.

'Who will pay?' Ratha asked.

'Rich ladies. Ladies who wash every day and smell like flowers. Ladies who never have rashes.'

Ratha thought that this was possible. On television he had seen rich people driving cars and living in big houses with sparkling swimming pools. But how would Thavery even begin, how would she save enough to leave Stung Meanchey?

Ratha followed Thavery along the wooden jetty that had been built before the lake became contaminated. He usually avoided the lake because the smell was as bad as the worst days at the dump, especially when the mud stretched for miles. Thavery put her sack down and lined up the bottles on the edge of the jetty. She had fourteen, a total she had proudly recited to Ratha. She knelt on the boards and put her arm over the side and filled each bottle with water, screwing the caps tightly into place.

At first Ratha just watched her fill a couple of bottles, then he grasped what she was doing, fished his bottles out of the sack, knelt down and began filling them too.

'The real trick is to save two bottles and put them at the top of the sack,' Thavery explained. 'When the pay clerk sees they're empty, he won't worry about the others. If you put the full bottles in the middle, inside a few plastic bags, he won't notice when they fall into the weighing cage. I always arrange my sack here, when no one's watching. He hasn't caught me yet. And don't use all the bottles. Six or seven are enough or the bag will weigh too much and he'll get suspicious. Save the rest for tomorrow, or for when you can't find any bottles. You'll make around two thousand riels extra a sack.'

Ratha smiled as he walked back beside Thavery. Now he knew why she always earned more than him, even though their sacks were the same size and were usually full of the same good rubbish. He was glad that they were leaving the stench of the sick lake behind them.

On the way to the weighing station, they stopped by Thavery's hut where they left a bag of bottles for another day. They made certain that two empty bottles were visible at the top, then went on. It was easier to lift the dead weight onto his back when Ratha could already feel the crispness of an extra two thousand riel note in his hand, a note he would be able to give to his aunt that evening.

*

Around three o'clock the trucks lined up at the gates of Stung Meanchey, waiting to get in. They were given directions to different parts of the dump, but they didn't always follow them. Once they were out of sight of the manager's hut, the drivers were able to unload almost anywhere.

Ratha and Thavery waited at the point where the main road split into three. A crowd of people gathered at the crossroads every afternoon, sizing up the parade of trucks. They would hesitate until someone spotted a truck they liked and rushed off after it. Others would follow, thinking that this man knew something about the source or the likely contents, so that a large throng of people might end up clamouring and pushing behind a single truck. If you were patient and went your own way, you were often rewarded with a much better haul.

Seng and the boys from the Eagles were standing just behind them. Ratha heard Seng say, 'Ratha's with that girl again. He's too scared to work with us boys.' Ratha glanced at Thavery and she smiled at him as if to say, it doesn't matter, you can go with them if you want. But he wanted to stay with Thavery. He hated Seng's taunts. Even if he went with the boys, Seng would still tease him about the rate at which he worked, he would still ridicule Ratha.

Just then Thavery spied one of her favourite trucks and said, 'That one.' Ratha nodded and they scampered after the truck as it rolled into the middle road. Racing after a truck was always exciting. There was the hope of finding something special and the joy of running hard so that you were right there when the truck began to tip. Ratha was quicker than Thavery, but she left the road before he did, cutting diagonally across the wasteland so that they arrived together just as the truck stopped. Other trucks were unloading all around them. For now, they had the whole truck to themselves.

Perhaps that's why Thavery did it. Perhaps she saw something – a coil of wire or a red scarf like the one she always wore. Maybe she glimpsed another naked doll. Or maybe she wanted to show the boys that she was brave too. Not long after the truck had raised its tipping structure and the load began to drop in a cavalcade of colours, Thavery stepped into the torrent of raining rubbish. Ratha had never done it and his aunt, Seak, had strictly forbidden him from ever doing something so dangerous, but some of the boys had jumped into the deluge and grabbed items of value before anyone else could claim them.

Thavery had her hook out and was reaching for something when the cyclo rolled into view at the top of the truck. It wasn't a complete rickshaw, just a battered seat with a torn hood and one mangled wheel. The rickshaw wobbled slightly, hanging there as a football does before it gains momentum and drops quickly. Once it left the truck, the rickshaw fell swiftly, turning over and over and striking Thavery in the small of her back. The seat hit her first, then the wheel and she fell forward into the rubbish. Everything seemed to stop for a moment just as the rickshaw propelled Thavery even further into the deluge.

Then Thavery screamed. The force of the falling rickshaw must have hurt her. She could easily be trapped beneath it, while all around her, the garbage fell. The garbage wasn't going to stop falling just because she was screaming.

Ratha should have reacted quicker; he should have done something sooner. Suddenly he was rushing forward, his arms raised to fend off the rubbish as he tried to reach her. Something wet and mushy landed on his head, something solid glanced off his forearm, but Ratha followed the shrill urgency of her screams and he found her. He put one arm under her back and one under her legs and lifted her backwards, fighting his way out of the falling torrent. Thavery was skinny and Ratha was strong, so the only difficulty was the rubbish that bounced and splattered onto them, coming at them without a break until they were out of its range.

Then Ratha heard the shouting. From all directions people came to their aid. Seak reached them first and together they laid Thavery down on her back.

Now Ratha understood why Thavery had screamed so loudly. She had fallen onto the point of her hook, which was sticking out of her chest. The hook was deeply embedded; perhaps it had gone in far enough to pierce her heart. No wonder she was screaming. Blood was pooling on her chest, then flowing off her and into the earth. Ratha grabbed the hook by the handle and tried to pull it out, but it wouldn't come. It was wedged in, stuck fast, like something buried under a mound of refuse. All Ratha managed to do was to make Thavery scream even louder.

Seeing Thavery lying there with the hook poking out of her chest as if she were some piece of garbage was the most horrible sight Ratha had ever witnessed. He wanted to free her, he wanted to stop the blood and to stop the screaming. Thavery's screams rose above the grinding din and the reversing alarms of the trucks. So terrible to hear your best friend scream like that.

People were talking in excited voices about what to do. The chain of Thavery's necklace had broken and three blue beads had shattered. She would be very upset about the necklace, but the glass beads could be replaced. Ratha was sure it could be mended. As one of the men lifted Thavery up, the string of beads slipped off her. Ratha picked the beads up, put them into his pocket and sprinted after Thavery.

Bo was carrying her, hook and all, towards the manager's hut. Seng's father ran ahead to ring for an ambulance, though everyone knew that an ambulance would never come for anyone at Stung Meanchey. Each step must have been a nightmare of pain, the hook jarring as Bo held her in his arms, her blood falling onto the road in large splotches.

Then she stopped screaming. Her scarf was tied snugly around her head and she was looking up at the sky. When Ratha saw her head roll to the side, he felt sick inside.

Bo carried her into the hut, but he came out straightaway. He put his hand on Ratha's shoulder, then hesitated. 'Thavery is dead,' he said, as if forcing himself to speak.

Ratha stood still and said nothing. The heat of the sun hurt his head. He reached into his pocket and found the beads there, puzzled by the feel of them in his fingers. Thavery had wanted to leave Stung Meanchey – but not like this, never like this. It wasn't fair. It was hard to believe that she was dead. That his friend was gone.

*

Life at Stung Meanchey went on. The trucks lined up every day. The garbage that was sifted and burnt was soon replaced by other garbage to be sifted and burnt. Some days Ratha worked on his own, determined to find the best rubbish, to be smarter than the other boys. Often he worked beside Kayrith and the boys from the Red Devils, hoping they would learn to like him and pass the ball more often.

His aunt was kind. She told him that she would be able to spare him sometimes, once her eldest boy was old enough to work. Maybe he could go to the French school and learn enough to become a hotel cleaner or a rickshaw driver. Ratha told Emile what his aunt had said and Emile suggested that there were other jobs he might train for, such as a motorbike mechanic, a cook, or even an accountant. But he would have to attend school regularly first.

Ratha listened to Emile and then thought about it while he scoured the dump for plastic and metal, for anything at all that could be sold. Each evening he played football for Kayrith's Red Devils against Seng's Eagles. They played on a road that ran along the western fence. It was narrow, but relatively clear of rubbish. The football was fierce, the arguments passionate, and each kick, each touch was keenly contested.

One evening when the fires were burning and the sky glowed orange and pink from the screen of smoke cast over the setting sun, Kayrith sent a cross into the penalty box. Ratha watched the ball spin towards him. This time he didn't hesitate. If only he'd been faster that afternoon, he might have saved Thavery. He sprinted forward, leapt into the air and met the ball with his tilted forehead. The ball volleyed past Seng and crashed into the imaginary net.

'Goal, goal,' Ratha yelled.

For once, no one argued. No one disputed the fact that Ratha's header was good.

Ratha raised both fists high. Now that he had finally scored, he would score again. Thavery had told him that he would score one day. She had been certain of it and she'd been right. Elated, Ratha jogged back past the hessian sack that marked the centre of the field.

WRITING WHAT YOU DO NOT KNOW

essay by Andy Kissane

It is hard to know exactly when or where the impulse for a short story starts. It seems reasonable to suggest that everything you do, everything you experience, everything you read can lead into writing. About four years ago I was teaching William Blake's poetry to first-year English students at the University of New South Wales in a course called Literature of Revolution. One of the themes of Blake's poetry that struck me then was his passionate concern for children and his representation of their plight in poems such as 'The Chimney Sweeper'. Many people would probably be surprised by the suggestion that a widespread belief in the merits of educating children that eventually led to the practice of compulsory schooling only developed in the late nineteenth century. Yet despite Blake's image of a young chimney sweeper who cries, *They cloth'd me in the clothes of death, / And taught me to sing the notes of woe*, child labour is still a fact of life for children in both developing and industrialised countries in the twenty-first century. Somewhere in my teaching of Blake was the germ of an idea that I would write about working children.

Work has been one of the focus areas of my writing, in poetry and fiction, for the past twenty years. I am not entirely sure why I am attracted to writing about work. It is a vital part of most people's lives, yet work has never had the same prominence in fiction as relationships or love. Initially, I channelled my interest in working children into a series of poems. One set in Victorian England dramatises the experience of a London match girl who inhales the deadly vapours of white phosphorus. One deals with the son of a cocoa farmer in Ghana who is carrying a sack of beans too heavy for his growing bones. One becomes a lament about the life of a boy selling enchiladas on a Mexican street. And one tells the story of a boy who scavenges to make a living in the Stung Meanchey garbage dump in Phnom Penh. Child labour, I wanted to suggest, is not merely a historical travesty, a thing of Blake's time, but something that is still with us today. I believe that one of the useful roles of writing is to protest, to describe the world as it is and provide a vision of how it could be. The global world is such a small place these days, with the evening news bringing stories from anywhere and everywhere into our living rooms, and there are no longer any taboo subjects for writers.

The poem that I became most involved in was the story of a boy working in a garbage dump and kicking a football when his working day was done. I write narrative poems and strongly believe that narratives belong in poetry. Many of our oldest narratives are poems – Homer's *Odyssey* and *The Iliad*, for example. Yet I felt there was more to be explored in my poem 'On Smoky Mountain' than I had realised. I had written about the physical process of working in a garbage dump and the struggle of daily life, and my poem also finished with Ratha kicking a goal, but it wasn't enough. I knew from writing the poem that Ratha's parents had died of AIDS, a fact I eventually left out of both the poem and the story. I wanted to investigate Ratha's relationships with others. His friendship with Thavery gradually grew in significance as I moved from poem to short story.

I have never believed in the mantra that you should write 'what you know'. This has become something of a cliché in creative writing classes, but it is not advice that I have ever endorsed. It strikes me as both misguided and pointless. There's no need to tell anyone this, because it's inevitable that your writing will involve some aspect of what you know. What most concerns you has a way of leaching out, even when you are not aware of it. Your psychology, your intonations, your word choices, your beliefs, your assumptions and your obsessions will surface without any deliberate attempt to mine them.

If you write about lives that you are initially ignorant of, then your writing has the potential to represent the depth, richness and complexity of the world. The whole process becomes a journey of discovery for the writer and the work is more rewarding for a reader. The key to writing what you do not know is imagination. And imagination, I believe, is something that everyone can develop. We already dream, while awake and while sleeping, and we possess the capacity to imagine what it is like to be someone else. Literature does this for us – it serves up poems, stories and novels built around the experience of others. It is perhaps literature's greatest strength, its most enduring quality, this ability to dramatise the thoughts and feelings, the experiences and lives of others. One of the most valuable aspects of writing and reading is the way it can take you outside yourself.

Still, I have never been to Phnom Penh or lived in a garbage dump and it is many years since I was ten years old. How do I know enough to begin, to take the first steps into a world that is foreign to me? I'm reminded now of the anecdote about Vikram Seth writing *A Suitable Boy*, getting one hundred pages into his novel about India in the 1950s, and realising that he did not know enough about his subject. So he goes and lives in a village in rural India for six months, even learning to make shoes by hand, something that one of the suitable boys subsequently does in his novel. But for most writers, family and work commitments preclude that sort of research, and even if you can travel, you might not know if your idea has legs, if it will actually work on the page.

Fortunately, the internet has made most forms of research so much easier. In writing 'Good Rubbish', I worked off photos, something I've done before when writing both fiction and poetry.

With a quick search, I located many photos on the net of the Stung Meanchey garbage dump and these images were easy enough to return to whenever I needed to prod my imagination. I found the work of the Polish street photographer, Maciej Dakowicz, most useful. His photographic library contained photos of the smoking mountain of rubbish, of swarming flies, of people crowding around trucks. There were photos of children in hats and scarves and children carrying hooks. There was a photo of a girl I came to think of as Thavery wearing a blue and silver bead necklace. Although other girls also wore necklaces, I could not find another one that was exactly like hers. And there were photos of boys playing football as the sun set and the smoke drifted over the dirt road. These photographs gave me enough information and enough inspiration to begin writing.

Over the last few years I have been writing contemporary short stories about families, about the relationships between men and women living in suburban Sydney. Somewhere in that time, I came hard up against the limitations of domestic realism, or what you might call the kitchen-sink story. I love stories about ordinary people, stories that don't depend on werewolves or grisly murders to grab the reader's attention, yet after a while the dynamics of ordinary lives can lack dramatic potential. This was not something I just noticed while writing; it was also something that struck me while reading contemporary short fiction. It might explain the prevalence of the war novel, for instance, and the attraction of politically turbulent times for novelists. If a character's life is at stake, then it's much easier to get some narrative drive into your story.

My favourite discovery of that time was Elizabeth Strout's Pulitzer Prize-winning short story cycle, *Olive Kitteridge*. The central character, Olive, is a maths teacher living in a small town in the United States and the book chronicles her life from her early adulthood to her old age. Although Strout's stories are grounded in domestic realism, I was struck by her mastery of the dramatic event. In the middle of the collection, the story 'A Different Road' begins with this sentence: 'An awful thing happened to the Kitteridges on a chilly night in June.' Olive and her husband, Henry, are taken hostage at a local hospital by two masked men hoping to procure drugs, and it is what they say to each other during this ordeal that changes everything. Similarly, Alice Munro's 'Dimensions', in *Too Much Happiness*, presents the story of a woman whose husband kills her children; while in 'Free Radicals' a widow's home is invaded by an escaped criminal. All these stories are powerful and memorable and they work because something happens. I have gradually come to believe that what stories need, more than anything, is for something to happen. This might sound like an obvious thing to say, but somewhere in the space and tension that exists between the everyday and the extraordinary, lies the makings of a great story. This is where heft and gravitas come from, and why, perhaps, some stories seem to matter so much more than others, until they become a part of your life.

Stories that build dramatically to a climax are the ones that stay with me. James Baldwin's classic story 'Going to Meet the Man' is a perfect example. There's an unforgettable lynching of a black man by a white mob that forms the story's climax. But what is remarkable about Baldwin's achievement is that he writes from the perspective of a white racist policeman, a perspective that is the antithesis of Baldwin's own experience as a black man and a civil rights activist in the 1960s. It's as if Baldwin set out to understand the very racism he was fighting against and to understand it from the inside. His story is insistently political, yet also compassionate and wise.

So I knew as the story of Ratha and Thavery gestated that something had to happen to one of them, that without Thavery being caught in a deluge of falling garbage, I wouldn't have a story. And it was just as important to me that 'Good Rubbish' didn't end with Thavery's death. I have a lot of respect for traditional structure and in classically structured stories a denouement follows on from the climax. Munro closes 'Dimensions' with Doree, the mother who has lost all her children, administering mouth to mouth to a boy who has just crashed his truck. This denouement introduces a sense of hope to a story that is insistently bleak and utterly captivating. In the same way, I wanted Ratha to have a sense of life beyond Thavery's death and scoring a goal seemed the best way to suggest that. One of the functions of the denouement is to offer the reader an opportunity to stay with the characters for a moment longer and to begin to reflect on the meaning and significance of the story. Good stories end well, they take the reader to a place they have never been to before. It is through this journey into the unknown that the story comes alive, for both reader and writer.

3825

'WEDLOCK'

Marion Halligan

Van and I always walked after school in a long diagonal across the playing fields then down Union Street into town. She lived in the police station at the end of the road, next to the bank, but after that I had to catch two buses to get home. Still I liked the slow walk and all the talking we did. Sometimes I went in and her mother fed us sponge cake with strawberries and cream. Her mum loved shopping and was always buying fabulous things for Van for practically no money, at sales; she haunted the shops until things were reduced. Bullied them into reducing them, often.

One of the things that preoccupied us at that time was whether men should be virgins at marriage, as had been made so plain to us women ought to be. We argued about this as we pottered across the playing fields. Finally Van said that if women were that would mean men should be, since there wouldn't be anybody for them to lose theirs on. I had just read a book about fallen women which took the rather novel view that many of these were really very nice girls who had stumbled upon hard times, and this was the cause of their falls from virtue. You'll see from this that I am talking about a long time ago.

Van was actually Vanessa, but she hated being called that because people only did when they were angry with her. Van-essa! they shouted. One afternoon she pointed back down the road. Go south, young woman, she cried. She'd been learning about Go west, young man! in history, but south was where we expected to make our fortune, in the great metropolis at the end of the line. A hundred miles away, by the Flyer, which was air-conditioned and didn't stop much. Sydney, that elsewhere that life was, that called to us so heartbreakingly.

What jobs will we get? I asked her.

Well, I reckon, retail. The beauty department of David Jones. It's kind of a humble start but we'll get on and start running the place. Or maybe fashion, we could become buyers.

I wasn't so sure about this. Van, yes. Tall, slender, willowy, long fair hair, that smooth pink and white matte complexion that never shines or blotches or pimples. Me, not. She worked in cosmetics in the local David Jones in the Christmas holidays; one look and you'd hire her. But I also thought I had a couple of years more of school to work it out, since I knew I had to stay until the Leaving. My mother was keen on a shorthand and typing course. I wasn't.

It was a Thursday, I remember, very hot. I waited for Van under the coral trees on the edge of the hockey field. When she came she looked prettier and smoother than ever.

I can't come with you today, Jill, she said, sorry, and skipped off. I was puzzled, but decided to walk home directly, in the opposite direction to her place, a long way but no need of buses. I was surprised at how early I got home. This became the pattern, Van always skipping off. Me puzzled, and disappointed; I thought she liked our talks. Then I discovered she was walking with a boy called Bruce, who worked in the ham and beef shop over the road from the police station. Well, he did a lot of the time, but seemed to have a couple of hours off in the afternoon. When they had a prisoner in the cells Van's mother had to make a meal for him, and sometimes Van went over to the shop to get something at the last minute. I suppose that's how she met him.

I missed our conversations. But walking home on my own I had time to think. I did find that quite pleasant after a while. Sometimes I had a few words with Van at school, but we did different subjects, so weren't in the same classes. We sat together at lunchtime, but in a crowd, no space for those old thrilling conversations about sex and what you should do.

I got quite addicted to walking home on my own, thinking about the day's stuff. Especially art history. The teacher had decided I was on her wave-length and now she kind of taught to me; she looked at me and mentioned things and gave the names of books in the library it would be a good idea to read. This day was cool, spring, there was a southerly breeze blowing in my face, I was thinking about the solidity of Giotto's figures compared with the linearity of Gothic sculptures on cathedrals like Chartres. I'd said that about the linearity of the sculptures and Miss Trewartha was very pleased. She lent me a book to take home. I know I can trust you to look after it, she said. It made my port even heavier but I didn't mind. When I got home Mum had a square thick envelope for me. Couldn't wait for me to open it.

It was an invitation. Mr and Mrs Roger King were requesting the pleasure of the company of Miss Jill Spencer at the marriage of their daughter Vanessa Denise to Bruce Trevor, only son of Mr and Mrs Brian Davey. At the cathedral. In two weeks.

Well, goodness me, said Mum. How old is she?

Sixteen. Like me.

Well.

At school, Van hissed in passing: I wanted you for bridesmaid – they wouldn't let me.

I thought she looked a bit peaky at the wedding. She had on a dress of lemon tulle, what they used to call a ballerina because of the length. Frothy it was. And not really her colour. The service took place in a side chapel. The dean, muttered the woman beside me. No white, no high altar. In her condition.

I thought of how her mother would have minded. On the sponge cake afternoons she was always poring over pictures in bridal magazines, asking our opinions about necklines, sleeves, veils, and what were the best colours for bridesmaids.

Van invited me to tea in her house high on the ridge, looking over the town and the sea. Rosy cups, silver teapot, a painted gilt coffee table. She showed me all her things. No chat about virginity or sex or how to behave. Dinner set, washing machine, six pairs of sheets, double bed. She displayed, I admired. Turned out Bruce didn't just work in the ham and beef shop. His family owned it.

I saw her again early in the winter, when the baby was born. A little girl, called Tiffany. The room in the hospital was stuffed with flowers, and that was what Van talked about. Who'd sent what, and how it took her all day to arrange them in the vases. Keep the water up, and stuff. Looking after them is a full-time job, she said. The baby was a bundle in the nursery, through a glass window, briefly.

Turned out I was the one went south. I got a scholarship and went to uni in Sydney, taking the wonderful Flyer that ran west behind the policeman's house and then turned right around and went south to the metropolis at the end of the line. I didn't get married for another ten years, and it was ten years after that I saw Van again. A high school reunion. She'd had five children by then and used a lot of French words because Tiffany had lived a year with a family in Paris. The whole family had spent a month there, in the cutest apartment in the Latin Quarter.

Zut alors, she said, after all these years. *C'est si bon* to see you. You look so well.

And you, Van.

Oh moi. It's Vanessa, by the way. I'm an old *maman* these days.

How's the ham and beef shop?

That was now a chain of delicatessens. And Bruce was on the council, likely to be mayor soon. They still lived on the ridge looking over city and sea, but in a much bigger house. After Tiffany three of the children were at school, Clinton the baby was at home with Van. Vanessa. She was pretty as ever, but not willowy any more. And the blond hair was a matter of art. The clothes were not those of an old *maman*.

And you, Jill?

I told her about my daughter, who was seven, about my marriage, which hadn't lasted.

Oh, poor you, she said.

No, not at all. It was a good thing. And now I have a friend, a companion, we don't live together, but we're very happy.

Ooh, good.

And I love my job. I teach art history at one of the Melbourne universities. It's my perfect thing. I love it.

That's nice.

You know how you talk to someone, and they smile prettily at you, and you can tell that they aren't taking the faintest notice of anything you say. It's not that they aren't hearing it, they could possibly repeat it word for word. But it doesn't touch their brain or heart. There's no attention being paid.

Fleur is keen to be a teacher, said Vanessa. After uni of course. She's in her last year at school. Tall with long black hair – would you credit it? She smiled a flirty smile. Maybe I'll get her to talk to you.

Well, she said, you're the one. You really went south. But, *zut alors*, I suppose someone's got to stay home.

BROWSING AROUND IN MY OWN HEAD

essay by Marion Halligan

I wrote this story for a competition. I dislike competitions and never go in for them. There must have been a compelling reason, probably a big prize. But there was also a theme, and I was keen to write a story about that, and so I did.

The theme was 'South'. I grew up in Newcastle, and anyone who has been to that city knows it has a very long main street (now dying, to the despair of traders), which runs parallel to the railway line, which runs parallel to the port, on a narrow strip of land that quickly rises to a steep hill, so that the cathedral, at the top, dominates the town as was the habit in medieval times. When you sail in to its dangerous harbour the cathedral is the highest thing. We went to town quite a lot, to the library, to the shops, buying dress materials and patterns, going to Lane and Trewartha for fine smallgoods. And it would always happen that the level crossing gates would close and a train go whooshing through. Sometimes the glorious Flyer, air-conditioned so no smuts, booked seats only, speeding off to Sydney, the great metropolis at the end of the line. But whatever sort of train it was, it made you long to be on the Flyer, going to Sydney. I would stand and stare after it, in a trance of desire. I can still feel it.

Milan Kundera wrote a novel called *Life is Elsewhere* which is a quotation from Rimbaud. In Newcastle in those days we knew the truth of the phrase, and we knew where elsewhere was. The railway line ran west along the harbour and then turned south. That was the south in my story, Sydney the city of plays and art galleries and the fascinating little shops of Rowe Street and David Jones. We did eventually get a DJs in Newcastle but Sydney was something else. Now I couldn't imagine anything worse than living in Sydney, but then … life was that poetic elsewhere.

That was the south. Two schoolgirls presented themselves as characters. I did have a friend with whom I walked across the playing fields, talking about momentous things like virginity, and she did live in the police station on a narrow sliver of land between the main street and the harbour. Her mother did make marvellous towering sponge cakes with strawberries and cream, and my mother didn't. She was tall and willowy and flawlessly complexioned, and I was good at art history. With a wonderful nurturing teacher. But we weren't Van and Jill. My friend went to university and got married shortly after she finished her degree, and I was her bridesmaid, along with her sister, all three of us in long stately dresses of a fabulously heavy white satin. That was quite a fashionable thing then. Her mother was in her element. The bride had fair hair, her sister a mass of red curls, and I was very dark brown. She began married life in a house with a quantity of bourgeois accoutrements, but didn't have children for some years. I got married shortly afterwards; despite my aunts thinking I was doomed to be a blue-stocking old maid all my life, I was only twenty-three. Seems quite bizarre now.

I did know of a girl at school, younger than me, who got married in the circumstances I gave to Van. And I saw her. I was at a function in the same rooms, waiting for the lift; it arrived and stopped at our floor, but was full of her wedding party. The doors opened, but none of us could fit in; it stayed for a while and then they closed, and it went on. The bride and groom were in the front, staring out from a frozen tableau, and I have never seen such naked misery in anyone's face. There she stood, in her lemon ballerina, looking unhappier than anyone deserves. It seemed to me such a cruel thing the dean and her parents colluded in, the grand marriage in the cathedral, but in the side chapel, the fancy reception, the lemon dress proclaiming her a fallen woman, in the manners of the time. They could have sent her to finishing school in Switzerland, or an aunt in the country, fine euphemisms both, but they chose to humiliate her in a public ceremony. Upholding the precept that marriage is the ideal fate for a woman, but at the same time mocking her. The word wedlock came to mind, with its curious sense of imprisonment, of incarceration and no key to undo it.

That marriage didn't last long, I believe. There was a key after all. But that wasn't the story I wanted. I gave Van, or Vanessa as she demanded, a continuing and reasonably contented time with her busy husband. A lot of marriages when I was young happened because they had to, as the expression went, and it seems to me now, looking back, that they had as much chance of being successful as less hasty ones. Shotgun marriages people called them, but the shotgun wasn't literal. Public opinion it was, in fact. Of course Vanessa is a strong-minded woman, she was determined to make a destiny for herself. I'd have loved to put in that scene with the lift, but Van refused humiliation, she constructed her own kind of glamorous life. Jill's seems to me more sympathetic, but I don't think a writer should play favourites with her characters.

I find that when I write a story it is only afterwards that I work out what is happening. This one of course is my perennial subject, love, marriage, birth, death (not much death here for a change), the absolute stuff of life, what really matters. What role chance, luck, destiny play in people's fates. The changing ideas of morality, manners, what matters, and yet how underneath the same preoccupations keep occurring. We thought as the sixties passed that we really had things worked out, that the pill gave women independence, that they could make their own lives as they desired. Now we are finding that fertility eludes us, that we don't have the control we thought we had. I don't do research for my stories, much, except to browse around in my own head. The past is a foreign country, they do things differently there, as L.P. Hartley so famously said. But it is a country that I once lived in, and I think it is important to remember what it was like; we don't want to be doomed to go through it again.

I have just been reading Elizabeth Jane Howard's first book in her *Cazalet* series, at ninety-three years of age she has just published the fifth. It evidently comes out of her own head. It's set in the late thirties; the question is, will there be a war, and it's a wonderful evocation of how little the fates of girls mattered in that era. Van and Jill some decades later are luckier, but Van's is the perennial female task of making the best of a bad deal.

It's quite a short story. As I recall, that's the demand of the competition. I like short stories, they are a challenge, getting something said in a small space. It didn't win; I wasn't surprised.

'TWILIGHT IN CAELI-AMUR'

Rjurik Davidson

The front of the house is overgrown with weeds, allowed to grow wild and free as they do on the hills behind Caeli-Amur. It's a grand old façade: pillars to the side of the double doors, which stand open; windows high on the second floor overlooking the street. In this part of Caeli-Amur, furnace trees line the sides of the road, their round bulbs overhead like lanterns in the night, collecting the heat in summer, emitting it in soft warm glows during winter. Now the sun's light has softened, so the cobble-stoned streets, the other grand houses with their balconies and domed roofs, the horse and carriage that I've just left by the side of the road seem faded.

With trepidation, one foot after the other, stopping and then again advancing, I enter Director Didion's house.

'Madame Didion, Madame Didion?' My voice echoes strangely around the entry hall with its two staircases that rise along each wall and join on the balcony above. Half-dead vines crawl from immense pots along the staircase rails, their brown leaves drooping, once-yellow candle-flowers trying desperately to pierce the gloom. They would have been magnificent once, befitting Director Didion's house, but now their withered trunks, knobbly and dry, remind me of dead bodies found high in the mountains. Candle-flowers are not among the plants that Didion created, but grow wild in certain marshes south of Caeli-Amur where at night, if you can bear the swarms of airborne insects and avoid falling into one of the treacherous bogs, the flowers light the air like a thousand magical flames scattered by some romantic god. The plants Didion designed always had a more dangerous beauty.

Rumours come to mind that I have not thought of for fifteen years, since I was a student following in his dark shadow at House Arbor, where jealous inferiors had concocted all kinds of spiteful stories: of Didion's hidden secrets and sexual depredations, of how he had taken other thaumaturgists' works and pretended they were his own, of how he favoured those students loyal to him, and excluded the brightest and the best.

I sneeze. Dust. Dust everywhere, a thin layer coating the floors, a powdery sea.

'Madame Didion?' Where is she?

Advancing beneath the staircases I pass into a corridor. Along the walls stand statues of bizarre creatures or gods, trunks sprouting from their faces, strange implements in hand. There are doors between the statues, and everywhere dead plants: once writhing silk-vines frozen and stiff, baby furnace trees in alcoves, their bulbs collapsed like empty bladders, desolate sticks emerging from dry pots. I try not to sneeze. Already my nose is becoming blocked.

'Madame Didion?'

I look through the door to my left, and there she is, seated on an intricately patterned couch. A table has been pushed up against the wall and fruit sits in a bowl, small orange and grey balls merging with each other. The smell of something rotting hovers in the air. A fat black cat scuttles beneath my feet and bolts down the hallway.

'Oh,' says Madame Didion, looking up towards me, her eyes tiny in her cadaverous face. 'Oh, I didn't hear you come in.'

'The door was open.'

'Oh, I know,' she says. 'I leave it open. I don't care.'

'But people might come in.' Images of thieves flash into my mind, with old Madame Didion helpless and frail on the couch.

'They don't,' she says.

'I suppose it's not the area for it.'

There's an uncomfortable silence for a moment and I shift my weight from one foot to another.

'Well, sit down,' she says irritably, as she would to a servant.

She has an extraordinary face, so old that it resembles a skull. The terribly thin skin has shrunk around the bones beneath. Red splotches dot her face and her hat casts a faint shadow, as if she's hiding herself from view.

I sit in a chair opposite her and neither of us speaks. She rubs one bony hand with the thumb of the other, purple veins running beneath the white skin. She doesn't look at me, but stares away at an angle towards the middle of the room. Another cat, this one with splotches of white and black and ginger, pokes its head around the corner of the doorway, examines the scene for a moment and disappears.

I want to ask her about the notebooks, to have her collect them so I can get out of the house, but it is too soon and it would be rude. I shift in my seat, unable to find a comfortable position. I have been warned: she does not want to give up the notebooks.

'Have you seen the house?' she asks, eventually.

'No.'

'Of course not. I keep thinking you were one of his colleagues. But I suppose you're much too young.' She says *his* as if he were here, as if he were still alive.

'I'm thirty-six,' I say in my defence.

'Yes,' she says, 'too young. He's been gone a long time, you know.'

Neither of us speaks. I search for something to say but only remember the reports of his affairs and his domineering temper: of how he struck his students with a knotted rope as he paced behind their chairs, leaving them stammering and red-faced and all the more likely to forget his formulae; and of how, as if to make up for these cruelties, he lavished them with opulent gifts of rare spices and pieces of ancient or lost technology.

'But even so,' she says in an unusually reserved manner, each word measured to reduce its effect, 'I remember him like it was yesterday. He was considered quite handsome in those days. A dashing figure, really.'

'I've heard only the best things about him,' I say. 'Stories of his brilliance.'

'Everyone liked him,' she says.

'Well, his achievements were enormous. We've all studied his theorems. His *Formulae for the Merging of Plant Species* is still the basic text in the House. And the stories of the new species – well, *Toxicodendron Didion* still protects the outer walls of House Arbor's palace.'

She sits up straighter as I speak and the edges of a satisfied smile play on her face. She must have basked in his triumphs for all those years and I thank the gods I'm not a woman. I couldn't bear to be excluded from House Arbor's laboratories, or from intrigues between the Houses. But then I'm a thaumaturgist and a man. One day I may even become Director.

'Come,' she says. 'Let me show you the house.' She stands and she seems smaller than I had first thought.

*

The house has vast expanses, great empty sitting rooms filled with coffee tables surrounded by delightfully embroidered chairs, now colourless beneath the dust, and some visibly mouse-eaten. Despite these holes the chairs are still arranged just so.

'He liked order,' she says. 'He liked things to be in their place.'

The dust overwhelms me again and I sneeze.

'You're sick,' she says.

'Oh, it's nothing.'

We pass through a ballroom, the walls lost in the gloom. Outside, the sun must be descending fast. 'We danced here. You should have seen the dances!' She leads me along grey corridors. 'We had many servants, you know. How the house was abuzz!' Kitchens lie off to the side. Somehow we end up in a wild and overgrown garden.

We follow a path that runs up the middle of the garden, which lies silently in the twilight. On both sides the weeds and grasses and bushes are impenetrable. Their colours take on an extra shade of blue-grey, an intimation of the approaching night. Some lean over us, their leaves brown now that it is late in the year. Many of these have dropped and are mounding up on the side of the path.

We come out into a central patio, two long lines of tear-flowers, fully five feet tall with heads like bloodied plates, running parallel to each other on its sides. Around them there are no weeds and the earth looks freshly turned and fertilised.

'Here are my flowers,' she says. As we approach, the flowers lean towards us and emit that faint wailing, like the cries of faraway children. Nectar slowly runs from their heads and down their petals. They recognise my thaumaturgical power – that is what they are designed to do. I stop and Madame Didion walks on. I note, with some surprise, that the flowers turn away from me and follow her, as she passes. Perhaps they have grown accustomed to her.

She reaches in, touches one and it shivers in delight, its petals undulating, calling her closer. I want to reach in and pull her away from its deadly calls but they are her flowers, and she has no doubt been here a thousand times. The only danger is to me.

As she walks along the rows, the tear-flowers, wailing and weeping, lean in further towards her, their heads beseeching her. A few notice me and turn indecisively before they lean back towards her.

A greenhouse stands on the other side of the courtyard, creeper vines covering it and enclosing it, passing through the broken panes, inside.

She passes along the other side of the patio and reaches out as the flowers there join the crying and weeping. 'They have a wonderful sound, don't they? Almost melodic, like an aria.'

'They do,' I say, even as I resist the pull of that mesmerising call. One does not lie down in a row of tear-flowers. No – they like their blood and bone.

'How long have you had them?' I ask.

'The same length of time they've had me,' she says, beaming. Her face is alive here – the flesh around her cheekbones suddenly rising, the eyes wider and sparkling. Suddenly she doesn't look so old.

'So how many notebooks are there?' I ask.

'Notebooks?' She raises both hands, palms upwards as if the notebooks don't matter and shrugs. 'Oh, three or four.'

'Oh,' I say, 'I thought there were six.'

She suddenly stops and turns towards the flowers, her back to me. 'Oh, yes,' she says almost inaudibly. 'Six.'

She steps closer to the flowers and by instinct I step towards her. The flowers lean in and nestle around her, caressing her face with their petals. Their nectar drips onto her shoulder. I should pull her away, but she is fine. And I don't wish to get too close to them. Already I feel like walking among them, listening to their mournful music, lying down beneath their flowing tears and closing my eyes. There I would never wake, but lie in that strange reverie, that semi-consciousness, as they suck me through their roots and up along their stems. I would lie half-alive, at their base, we will have become one living creature – the flowers and I.

She steps backwards. 'Let me show you the rest of the house.'

'But the notebooks…'

'Ah yes,' she says. 'Come on then.'

*

Somehow, retracing our steps, we reach a vast dining room, the table set for a banquet. There are no notebooks to be seen.

'There he is!' she says. 'Magnificent, isn't he?'

The portrait shows a stern man, powerful. He has grey hair and an angular, harsh face. His eyes stare out, all fire and passion. It is painted in the style of the forties, so there's something unreal about it: the power and the sternness of the portrait reside simply in its form. House Arbor has always used that style, and still does. I try to reconstruct what he would have looked like, to distil the reality of the man from the pompous façade of the painting.

'Yes,' I say. 'Magnificent.'

'He was a good man. He served House Arbor all his life. He was loyal, to all of us, and look, he built us this house and he gave us three wonderful children. And they gave us grandchildren. What more can you ask for?'

'Your children. They work for the House?'

'No, they are up north, in Varenis.'

'So you never see your grandchildren?'

'Oh no. Anyway, I wouldn't want them to come here. I'd scare them.'

'Well, you are quite … powerful,' I say.

'I think they'd be scared by how old I am,' she says, ignoring me.

'So what are these notebooks, I mean, are they all about thaumaturgical anabolism and hybridisation?'

She looks up at the portrait and then away again as she speaks. 'He practically invented it, you know. He would retreat into the library, all kinds of philosophy and theory spread out on the desk. You should have seen him. And the delight of discovery! When he first recognised how to augment the speed of plant growth by the connection of previously unrelated thaumaturgical formulae. The way, suddenly a whole new world opened up in his mind and everything seemed wondrous and strange.' There's something about the way she stares off into the distance as she speaks that takes me aback.

'And then later,' she says, 'he found he could use some of the same equations not just to speed up the growth of plants, but animals too. And why not humans?'

'But it was never done,' I say.

'Who knows what the House did? He was a theoretician; he did all the formulation of the initial foundations of that branch of thaumaturgy. He was an innovator. He created new plants, but they were mainly for theoretical research. What Arbor did with that knowledge, it kept to itself. Perhaps you know – you're a thaumaturgist for the House.'

'I don't know,' I say, and she smiles, knowing that I could not say even if I wanted to. She nods and looks back up at the portrait.

'Talented…' she says slowly.

She turns suddenly towards me, and leans in, an innocent look on her face, pleading and beckoning, almost siren-like. 'Does the House really need them? I mean, after all these years?'

I bet she used that look to seduce many a man when she was young. It's an unfair thought, but it comes to me just the same.

'Perhaps you could make copies…' I say, but the absurdity of it strikes me. House Arbor takes what it considers its own.

She curls her lip, and again I feel like a servant. 'Does a painter make do with duplicates of a painting? A writer with copies of his first manuscript? An original is an original. Anyway, these are in his handwriting, a piece of him. You think a copy can reproduce him?'

Foolishly I stand at attention, like a chastened child, but her voice softens again. 'I mean … they're the last thing I have to remember him by.' Behind those words I hear the entire edifice she has created, the entire world of her life and her place in it, her status defined by her relationship to him, the innovator, the originator.

I look around the room and back to the painting. He seems to be challenging me, daring me to betray his memory. I look at Madame Didion and she shrinks backwards, turns away and says, 'They're in the library.'

She stands still for a moment and then, in a broken voice says, 'Excuse me for a moment.' She shuffles quickly back into the corridor where she sobs, high and uncontrolled. I remain still before the portrait of her dead husband as she weeps on the other side of the wall, emitting low and uncontrolled guttural sounds and great heaving breaths. We stay in place, like mirror images of each other, as the house descends into yet a darker shade of gloom. Finally the sobbing stops and shortly afterwards she comes back into the room.

'I'm looking forward to showing you the library,' she says. 'I'm sure you'll like it.'

*

It's a whole wing, the library, with stairs rising to antechambers, little grottos filled with ramshackle shelves, some entirely covered with grassy mould or lichen, as if thin green blankets have been thrown over them. But no! I think. Not the books! What wonders could be lost in there?

I follow her into a splendid circular domed study, with a massive desk made of oak resplendent under the glass ceiling, the sky now the darkest shade of blue. The dust has taken this place too but Madame Didion is oblivious to it.

Everything has a ramshackle feel, disorganised and cluttered. Piles of yet more books stand beneath the shelves, towers threatening to fall onto each other. Scrolls form a great sea to one side of the desk, which is cluttered with tiny statues and fountain pens and ink wells and mechanical watches and incense burners and other assorted knick-knacks. It is so disorderly.

'Are the notebooks here?'

She looks away, breathing rapidly, her small chest rising and falling. I hope she doesn't cry again.

Madame Didion looks back at me for a moment. Her gaze holds mine and we wait, as if to see whether the other will break. I cannot ask her again for the notebooks.

'Here they are,' she says finally, and reaches up to a book-filled shelf. She pulls down two large books. Didion's famous notebooks. I look at them, with their thick leather binding. Dust makes the brown leather appear grey.

She holds them in her hands, and rubs her bony little thumbs over the soft leather and the fine engravings, once silver but now merely residual. She rubs the books the same way she rubbed her hands earlier.

'You'd better take them,' she says, but instead of giving them to me, she places them on the desk, away from me, and steps backwards. A parchment sits on the desk; my eyes strain in the darkness to make out a spidery handwriting laying out formulae, equations, paragraphs of reasoning. Beside the parchment lie the pages of a manuscript. Neither is dust-covered.

'Six?'

'Oh yes, the others are up there on the shelf. You'd better get them.'

We stand there, in some sort of counterpoint. Perhaps I could only take four, then at least she'd have two left. But I know it's impossible. The items will be taken to the House Arbor Palace, itemised, shelved, studied by the House Thaumaturgists. Dissertations and critiques will be written, lectures and debates organised. Careers will be made. I must take them all or questions will be asked.

'It was you, wasn't it?' I ask.

'I don't know what you're talking about, dear.'

'You were the one, not him. You. I saw the way the flowers leant in towards you. Your flowers. And these: your notebooks.'

'Oh, don't be ridiculous.' She turns away, looks for no reason towards a shelf on the wall. 'Don't be silly,' she says again, quietly.

But even now I can see the sheen of thaumaturgy around her. I've studied Carel's *Ontology of the Thaumaturgical Universe* and Taslin's *Structure and Augury*. I can read the powers in the air; I can put together formulae and equations, one after the other, connecting and intertwining them just so. I can see her aura now that I'm looking for it, wavy and old in the darkness that encloses us. Her pride will keep her secret until death, and I will not betray it.

'Take the books and I'll show you out,' she says.

She leads me through that massive and empty mansion, the dust billowing about us. It is almost completely dark now. Dead plants emerge from the gloom like ghostly relics of some ancient desert and the doors gape like even blacker holes in the night. When we come to the entrance hall, the candle-flowers on the vine try desperately to emit a tiny yellow light.

'Aren't they beautiful,' she says, standing next to the grand staircase.

I try not to sneeze as I make my way to the entrance doors. I pass through them and look back. She stands there, beside the half-dead vine, like a ghost herself.

'Shall I shut the doors?'

'Don't bother,' she says. 'I don't care.'

'People might come in.'

'They don't.'

I nod (though I doubt she sees it in the darkness) and turn away.

'Why don't you come again?' she says. 'We've had such a lovely time.'

I turn back. 'Yes. Perhaps I will.' I feel guilty saying it, and as if it will make a difference I add: 'I think I might.'

And then I turn and head out of Director Didion's house and up to the street. Stars twinkle between quickly moving clouds. The horse and carriage stands silent on the street: the horse's head down and unmoving, the driver waiting patiently as is proper when transporting a thaumaturgist of House Arbor. The bulbs on the furnace trees have begun to glow, and even now, as autumn is upon us, I can feel the faint warmth emanating from them, like little fires hanging in the night. It will not be long now until winter.

IN DEFENCE OF SLOW FANTASY

essay by Rjurik Davidson

Modern fantasy descends from two significant traditions. The first is the tradition of ancient myth: the Greek and Viking myths, sagas like the Finnish *Kalevala*, or the those of the Hindu pantheon. Tolkien was the dominant figure in the modern incarnation of this tradition, having borrowed from many of these sources.

The second tradition emerges from the pulp magazines of the first half of the twentieth century. Pulps like *Weird Tales* pumped out dashing tales of adventure – replete with racism, sexism and neo-fascism – by people like Robert E. Howard. Quite often these were stories of colonialism or westerns rewritten with fantasy (or science fiction) trappings. This tradition can be discovered nowadays in movies like *Avatar*, a western in space.

Both these sources encourage a particular kind of story, replete with external action, filled with heroes and heroines, gods and magic, epic battles, and so on. When reading fantasy, then, one comes to expect a certain kind of narrative, with certain kinds of events and certain kinds of protagonists. This is part of the reason some don't consider fantasy as 'real' literature, though it's a reading that is not only unfair but has its own ideological assumptions, most obviously that 'genuine' fiction can only be the province of the 'internal psychological' narrative, its concerns those of the bourgeois family and its trials (affairs and petty betrayals).

I've always resisted the notion that fantasy cannot be 'real' literature. This requires a double refusal.

First, one must refuse the traditions of fantasy itself, and to a large extent the expectations of much of its readership. One must refuse the adolescent concerns of hero-driven action stories, the clear divide between good and evil, the naturalisation of feudalism, racism, sexism, and so on.

Second, one must refuse the claims of those who see fantasy as only *capable* of expressing those adolescent concerns. One must show that it is a literature capable of addressing issues such as race, gender or sexuality, of meaning in everyday life.

My project was always to try to write stories that were both 'real' literature and yet still irreducibly fantasy. It's a dangerous project, for you risk alienating yourself from the 'literary types' who see fantasy as sub-literature. You also risk alienating yourself from fantasy readers who want only to read epic narratives of adventure.

Still, it's a project worth pursuing.

About five years ago I started to write what could be called 'slow fantasy' (and 'slow science fiction'). I wanted to reverse the commonly held expectations of action-oriented fiction. Instead of the open physical action of a 'hero', I wanted everything to be occurring beneath the surface of the story, in the subtext. I wanted to write stories where the action was not a hero cleaving down a villain, but a word or phrase spoken by one of the characters, or a gesture, or something left unsaid – and yet remain definitively fantastical. The characters would live in a world closer to our own. Their concerns would be adult concerns: problems of politics and career. Slow fantasy was to be the sort of imaginative fiction Raymond Carver might write. It's a project that develops the ideas of the 'New Weird' writers who emerged in the early 2000s, and the 'New Wave' science fiction writers of the 1960s, though I'm not aware of many fantasy writers pursuing this particular 'slow' direction.

I'd already tried this with the science fiction story 'Domine' (reprinted recently in *The Time Travellers Almanac*), and I set my mind to working on the fantasy equivalent.'Twilight in Caeli-Amur' was my first attempt.

*

The story itself is simple. There are three sections. In the first the unnamed narrator arrives to collect the notebooks. In the second he registers there is something unusual about Madame Didion. The final section shows the moment of revelation.

I set myself several technical challenges. To begin with, certain things are withheld from the reader. It is a story of façades, a story of masks and mirrors. No one openly says what they think, or what they know.

Withholding information is a dangerous technique, because the author runs the risk of annoying the reader. There are a couple of moments where the narrator indicates that he knows something, but doesn't let the reader in on it. At its best, this can work a little like an unconscious realisation, where it's only after the fact that some hidden part of you knew something was up. At its worst if appears like authorial manipulation.'Why won't he just spit it out?!'

On the other hand, a great deal of story writing is about *when* you give out information and *what* information is given. The idea in 'Twilight in Caeli-Amur' is that the reader should suspect that Madame Didion is the real source of power before the narrator states it.

In a 'traditional' fantasy story, Madame Didion might refuse to hand over the notebooks. She might set a creature – the flowers perhaps – onto the narrator. There might be a conflict, a fight, between them.

I preferred the change of the story not to be in the order of things, but in the narrator's and the reader's minds. Caeli-Amur will continue on as it always does, but the narrator – and perhaps the reader – will see the world differently.

Many short stories have three characters, a protagonist and two characters pulling that protagonist in different directions. In 'Twilight in Caeli-Amur', the third, missing, character is that of Didion himself. He is, of course, a classic patriarchal figure, ambitious and narcissistic. You've probably met many like him. This kind of person is encouraged by our culture.

In this way the story is a critique. Not only of that kind of character, but of the society that holds Didion up as hero, and that fails to see Madame Didion.

In a certain sense, the story is a version of Virginia Woolf's 'Shakespeare's sister'. For those unfamiliar with this term, the idea is that Shakespeare's sister (or wife perhaps) might have been an equally talented writer, but because of social constraints could never publish under her own name. What could she do? Perhaps, we might speculate, she was the real author of the plays and sonnets and convinced her brother to pretend they were his. From this perspective, 'Twilight in Caeli-Amur' is – or so I hope – a feminist one (Madame Didion is not even her real name!).

The old epic fantasies always had trouble with feminism. Action heroes were inevitably male until at least the late 1960s, when the genre stereotype was occasionally reversed (just as *Buffy the Vampire Slayer* reversed gender stereotypes for film and TV in the 1990s). That kind of reversal is little more than a playful moment of 'girl power'. There's not much depth to it, for it relies on a kind of liberal individualism that leaves everything else untouched. The structures of power can't be represented in such narratives, because those very structures would hold a female hero down. She could not overcome them by individual will alone, which is the very point of 'girl power'.

In any case, I wanted my slow fantasy characters to have the everyday concerns of 'real' people. Where then did I seek inspiration?

*

Only once have I based a story on a particular living person. Usually my characters are pure inventions, or at best composites of characteristics taken from real people. 'Twilight in Caeli-Amur' was thus an exception. In this case, Madame Didion is based on my grandmother.

At the time I wrote the story, my grandmother was a frail old woman of over ninety-five. I need not describe her – for she was just like the character in the story – except to say that she was a unique personality. Powerful and at times scathing, she was in equal measures humble and restrained. She had led an extraordinary life, having travelled through India in the 1950s or 1960s on her own, before there were backpackers' trails. She spoke or read something like thirteen languages. She was highly educated and spoke in an aristocratic English drawl. All the time she insisted there was nothing out of the ordinary.

There was something touching and tragic to this modesty.

Although she was born to an upper middle-class family in Belfast nearly a century earlier, she ended up living in a little dilapidated house on the outskirts of Melbourne. Few people visited her. Few knew who or what she was. One of my regrets is that I did not spend more time with her during those last years.

Madame Didion is not, of course, my grandmother. She is an invention who embodies the spirit of my grandmother and was set off on her own course, doing her own things. Whenever an author bases a character on a real person, that character is *never* actually that person.

Part of the world that Madame Didion passes through is a distinctly fantasy one.

*

The single image that probably stays with the reader is that of Madame Didion standing by her flowers. The flowers – ah, those deadly and beautiful things. The story is still irreducibly fantasy, a genre that allows for fantastic possibilities. The author's task is to pick images or scenes, events perhaps, which can represent the story's themes. Crucially, the story should not be able to be easily rewritten without the fantasy elements.

'Twilight in Caeli-Amur' wouldn't have the same effects without that image, for there would be no way to capture Madame Didion's mastery of the flowers and the mysterious powers of 'thaumaturgy', that fusion of science and magic. We would not have a sense of Madame Didion's *power* without that scene, where the narrator looks on, afraid.

It's the image that stays with me: our narrator, too afraid to approach, watches as Madame Didion stands close enough for some of the flowers' nectar to drop on her shoulder. She loves those flowers and the flowers love her. In these small, subtle moments, I hope to show what fantasy – slow fantasy – can do. It's a literature capable of capturing our adult concerns and dilemmas, a genre that can do this with its own style and power.

'NHILL'

Patrick West

As I had hoped, when we arrived at the lake we were the only people there. Neither of us had seen any other cars at the place where the road ended and the desert began. Yet perhaps there was another way in we didn't know about, or somebody had decided to camp overnight on the shore of the lake. Somebody who didn't have a car, perhaps. But there was no one.

The evening before, over a shared ice-cream dessert at the motel restaurant, my wife had told me that she would be going to bed as soon as we were finished, to be rested for our early start the next morning. Though worn out myself by the half-day drive from Melbourne, I had stayed up for some time after her, getting together the things we would need for our trip into the desert, estimating distances and times.

Our room was next door to the reception area. The manager had his TV turned up loud and kept switching irritatingly between the channels. There had been a movie on, and the local news, and it wasn't until after the movie that I had turned off the main light. Getting into bed myself, next to my wife, I lay on my back and thought of the pair of empty fish tanks on the manager's desk. And then I think I took a long time falling asleep, because when our alarm clock went off it seemed as if the movie was still going on inside my head.

There had been no lights shining in the motel complex when I eased the room door closed behind us and unlocked the passenger side of the car for my wife. The only artificial illumination came from the frosted lamps around one side of the swimming pool, which made the water bright green. I had remembered thinking, though, upon our daylight arrival, that I had never seen water so blue. There had been clothes pegs on the bottom that afternoon. Children were diving for them.

Some of the fainter stars had been dimming out as we drove along the road that would soon veer right and become the main street of the town of Nhill, Victoria. Our motel was at about the point towards the end of a long stretch of highway where the speed limit begins to be lowered on white-and-black signs. We both saw a rabbit in the headlights.

A few minutes after we had departed the silently sleeping motel, my wife spotted the turn-off to the Little Desert before I did. Her vision was much keener in the pre-dawn light. The road to our destination ran alongside the railway tracks on the edge of Nhill. Our tourist map showed us that halfway to the desert the road and the tracks would diverge, meet again, then finally part for good. I slowed down to take the left-hand turn.

While the light continued to increase and alter, she had been the one to say the morning had broken. A sliver of sun flashed across my rear-vision mirror as we parked on a slope of dew-dusted earth. I turned off the engine. For the first time that morning it was perfectly quiet.

For a while we hadn't even been sure if we were really in the desert or not. Then we came to a turnstile in a short run of wire fencing, and we knew. We had arrived. The turnstile had a counter attached; as we went through, the white numbers noiselessly turned over. It was probably part of someone's job to note how many people went into the desert. Perhaps this information was important. I couldn't help thinking about those people who deliberately went around the fence, or used the turnstile more than once. My wife must have read my mind. She had said quietly, perhaps it all evens out in the end.

That had also been when we first noticed the real sand mixed with the soil beneath our feet, and that the Little Desert mainly consisted – the vegetation falling away – of a serried formation of low rises and shallow dips. We were now into a new landscape, walking across the first of its modest plateaus, incongruously headed for water.

Tucked into my shirt pocket was a map of the desert produced for walkers, and we weren't long in our progress towards the lake before the cartographic marks – like the diminuendos and crescendos on a page of music – became signs we could interpret. The map gave the lake a neat edge, filled in with a colour that by convention indicated deep water. But my wife and I had speculated that at that season, and at the very centre of the desert, the lake would be a salt lake. Its water would be shallow and its shore uneven, we had guessed. And we were right.

The whole morning, from the surface of the path and from the rest of the ground, the air had been rising in warm waves. What little there was of copper-coloured, needle-like grass had been the first to respond. An hour later, the same waves had brushed around our faces, slowly continuing to ascend, moving through black and blond hair like fingers of gentleness. This was a sensation we hadn't felt before, out there in the relative flatness of the Little Desert. And then, when our watches showed that it was almost noon – hour and minute hands about to touch the twelves on our wrists – we noticed again how peculiar nature is.

Although there wasn't a breath of wind, the few trees at first appeared to be straining against their confinement in the earth, all of themselves rejecting the land from within.

The next moment, however, this had curiously seemed not to be happening. Precisely the absence of even the weakest breeze now manifested itself as decisive, as if the trees that we could see here and there on the landscape, not needing for their equilibrium to be rooted and heavy and thus not being so, were no longer rebelling against their connection with the lowest part of the visible desert, but were touching it with only the smallest possible touch, nothing of themselves actually buried into the loose soil.

As if roots had withdrawn completely into trunks, as if something had turned completely and utterly around, as if the few trees were held up sheerly by the rising air – a delicate balancing act – and into its cloud-headed warm waves.

I had walked with my binoculars around my neck, seeing two eagles. Or perhaps the same eagle twice.

At times, the silence was extreme.

There had been low signs by the side of the path at irregular intervals, sometimes three or four clustered together. On them were descriptions of the interesting aspects of the desert and its life. Here were indicated two trees that had grown into each other in a cleft of rock, and become one; there, the same thing had happened, but with one of the trees having died. A few of the signs had referred to rainfall or temperature change in the Little Desert's unique microclimate. Others said that at this spot one could often see a particular bird or furtive animal. My wife had told me that the signs looked like church lecterns springing from the ground, or tombstones made to resemble open books. (A rare parrot we read about had last been seen in 1961, by N. Green.)

Our route to the lake had taken us through a part of the desert supporting very little in the way of scrub or other plant growth. The ground had to it what my wife called an angry tone. In places the sand gathered in drifts deep enough for our legs to disappear up to the bare flesh of our calves.

At the point where our walkers map told us that we would arrive at our lunch spot by the salt lake in just under an hour, we had found ourselves on a slightly higher plateau, where the fine sand gave only a few grains of cover to the shale beneath. In view before us was an expanse of clumpy bushes of a bleached-green colour: a prospect of palest olive. Obviously we were on the edge of fertile soil. It had almost looked as if we might walk, from where we were, right across the top of the scrub, to the next low rise; although by careful observation, if nothing else, we knew we couldn't. The surface of the scrub was even and uninterrupted, but the smallest bird to alight on it sank beneath the feathery leaves and tips. Sank to fly out of the scrub's surface bafflingly elsewhere (the same bird? or another?).

I had related to my wife what I knew about a certain type of mixed bush-growth in western Tasmania, described in forestry literature, which was often able to sustain – for considerable distances – the weight of people who simply wanted to walk above the land for a while. My wife had only grimaced in response. She was becoming tired; the comparison, furthermore, was a vague one. The scrub we were faced with then was not only unable to support us, but allowed no sort of passage through its web of lower branches either. We were therefore forced to make a long detour, by the fainter trail around its stunted-grass perimeter, in order to regain our path to the lake on the further side.

For no known reason, we had each taken a different way from the other. Tiny desert mice and prodigious desert rats were in shadowy motion within the scrub, chittering among themselves without regard to size or species. Under blazing sun, it had felt nevertheless as if I were looking into darkest night.

There was orange peel on the ground where the main path took up again: the first sign of recent intrusion that either of us had seen.

We had caught sight of the salt lake just a little later than my planning had allowed for.

As I had hoped, when we arrived at the lake we were the only people there. Neither of us had seen any other cars at the place where the road ended and the desert began. Yet perhaps there was another way in we didn't know about; or somebody had decided to camp overnight on the shore of the lake. Somebody who didn't have a car, perhaps. But there was no one.

Across the lake we could see three waterbirds still as statues, a little way in from the opposite shore. They did not disturb at all the few centimetres of water they were at rest in. It gave out almost nothing, that salt water: without movement and shallow at every point. Reflections from the surface of the lake were mixed with the appearance of its bottom. It was difficult even to be sure about what sort of a body of water we were looking at. An oversized puddle? Ridges of land that began well back in the desert around us continued out into the lake as thin fingers of earth, like the spokes of a gigantic wheel, which dropped beneath the surface only when almost to the middle. They were the ribs of the Little Desert, I had thought to myself, and this was its watery heart.

The ducks' heads were nestled comfortably into the plumage of their napes. Nothing stirred. All between our words was without noise. For a moment, I almost believed that I could watch the silence that surrounded us. It had been as if the visible landscape – the few trees, the copper-coloured, needle-like grass – was listening to what we said, finding it eventually acceptable, and allowing our utterances to pass back into the quietness unhindered.

We had arrived. The two of us. At a heart of salt.

It was difficult to have to quit the lake's irregular and pockmarked shore so quickly, now that we were finally where we wanted to be. But it was past the time to have our lunch, we were both tired, and the path to the nearest shady place to eat and rest was going to take us a short distance away from the lake. My wife and I had removed our hiking boots and socks to test the temperature of the water; now we needed to sprint across the burning ground to the spot we had decided upon almost immediately after our arrival. Even several long steps from the edge of the salt lake, however, the sand was cool and moist.

Water usually darkens whatever it touches, and I have read somewhere that this proves it is not really crystalline but pure black, which is to say that it makes things black by an invariable law of change and resemblance. Nowhere in even the immediate vicinity of the lake, however, did the colour of the sand vary from the salty whiteness presented by other parts of the Little Desert. Even the thin fingers of land had a pale and glazed hue. More than likely the same went for the bottom of the lake, although through the shallow depths of the water we couldn't tell for sure.

As we opened our backpacks, ate our sandwiches, splashed our cold drinks into our mouths, we talked about such things. A million days of evaporation, my wife said through a mouthful of bread and mortadella, had done something to the Little Desert to make its surface impervious to the effects of water. An element in the rain was not taking on the sand, I had thought without saying.

When we had finished our lunch and felt rested again, we went back to the shore of the lake. The ducks were exactly as they had been upon our arrival. We stood on the damp sand and watched over them.

There was nothing mystical about the scene in the end. No unworldly presence suggested itself in the shallow water. There was only the salt lake precisely as it was, and a sky that all day had not been disturbed by an aeroplane. All the same, it was a place (the lake, the sky, the whole sense of it all) that you didn't want to treat like more familiar places.

When we made up our minds to go it was in sadness. A single duck's cry carried to our ears with almost no volume at all, the smallest increment imaginable before deafness begins.

*

Our return hike through the desert took much less time than the journey we had begun just as the sun was rising. We walked quickly, shut out distractions, only parted company once, each of us taking the grassy route around the pale olive expanse of scrub that the other had taken when we were still making our way towards the unknown salt lake. Our voices sang out across the even surface of the bushes so each other might hear, and perhaps be comforted.

The sign requesting visitors to leave the Little Desert around either end of the short run of wire fencing is easy to miss, as we had been guilty of, when proceeding in the direction of the water. We couldn't pretend we hadn't seen it now, coming back. Climbing over the turnstile, however, would save us any further time today in the desert. It looked easy enough. Together we took hold of one of the metal arms.

Perhaps it was some chemistry of our four hands simultaneously gripping this object (palms of a man and of a woman) that made it suddenly turn the wrong way, shift backwards without warning from the salt-lake side. Whatever the reason, in an instant we were ejected from the desert, and needing to pick ourselves up. My wife's pants required dusting and I was happy to oblige. Checking the white numbers – the dry bodies of insects caught between the discs of the meter – I realised, by some fluke of memory, that they were exactly as they had been after our entrance at dawn.

This seemed to mean two things: our inelegant departure had not registered on the counter; and no one else had come through. We had always felt ourselves alone that day. Yet perhaps the white numbers had, in fact, surreptitiously registered our exit, had clicked back (once? twice?) while we tumbled out of the Little Desert, and either a single person or a couple, whom we had never seen, had entered after us. Perhaps they were still in there.

Starting the car, I suddenly thought that our trip to the salt lake was somehow never to stop happening. And then I had the impression that I was having the same thought distinctly and clearly again.

*

The next morning, we ate breakfast sitting on the double bed in our room. A stray leaflet advertising the house-museum reputedly the Nhill home of the nineteenth-century romanticist poet John Shaw Neilson slipped between the sheets. Afterwards I swam several slow laps of the nauseatingly chlorinated pool – one clothes peg still winked from the bottom.

Melbourne half a day away. In her reclined seat, my wife recited the back of our tourist map. The Little Desert and the Big Desert are two unique geographical and climatic regions; each is different from the adjoining countryside, and each is different from the other. She pointed to the north, without turning her head my way, and said that the Big Desert was less than a hundred kilometres – pointing vaguely northwards, with splayed fingers – over there...

That afternoon, turning into our street in the suburb of St Kilda, I glimpsed again the brilliant green waters of Port Phillip Bay. How could such intensity ever seem so deep to us again? My wife started telling me that everything was going to be fine in a little while and I needed to listen to her with great care. Every word she used sounded as though travelling to me through both water and sand, and from much further away than she really was.

WRITING 'NHILL': THE SHORT STORY AS STILL LIFE

essay by Patrick West

Fanaticism? No. Writing is exciting
    and baseball is like writing.
        You can never tell with either
            how it will go
            or what you will do.

'Baseball and Writing'[1]
Marianne Moore

Marianne Moore knows what she's talking about! Not knowing where it will lead me is why I love writing so much, and why I love the short story in particular. In my experience, the short story is roomier than the novel.

This is not the paradox it might seem. Ideas that would fritter away to nothing over the extended journey of the novel, or get pushed over the edge of the novelist's fictional world, often fit perfectly with the more condensed and concentrated time-space of the shorter form. Less, in this case, is certainly more.

However, unlike poetry for example, the short story must by definition relate a story, be it through telling, showing, or an alliance of these. Its potential for experimentation is thus limited, or as I would prefer to say, framed, by its built-in commitment to narrative.

Such a combination in the short story of almost unlimited creative possibilities with the strict requirement to 'tell a story' offers opportunities to attempt a narrative about just about anything, including subjects, notions or fancies that might appear actively resistant, not just to the construction of a story, but to writerly expression itself. And this is where things can turn decidedly strange.

Let me tell you a story about a story. I wrote the first version of 'Nhill' when I was in my early twenties. But it was twenty or so years before I realised that, over the course of its rewriting, I had not (just) been doing what I thought I had been doing.

I thought that I had only been writing, and endlessly revising, a story about the relationship difficulties of a young couple trekking through the Little Desert on the outskirts of Nhill in the Wimmera region of Western Victoria.

My multi-layered use of the past perfect tense in this story was intended to convey a sense of the (narrating) present being *inevitably* cut off from the (narrated) past – as if this, in itself, were the cause of the couple's mis-communications. Similarly, the choice of first-person point of view was meant to suggest an entrapment within the self of the narrator (something also expressed by the extensive repetitions, as if all that could be said was what had been said so often before). Again: the absence of direct speech was used to underscore how the man and woman don't really talk anymore.

(I have sometimes sensed readers' disapproval at how little direct speech many of my early stories contain. However, in her review of 'Nhill', in *Australian Book Review* in 2006, Delia Falconer went the other way, observing that 'Nhill' 'would be perfect but for its last line'.[2] That last line was three words of direct speech! No work of art is every really finished; sometimes it takes public feedback, like Falconer's, to make it less un-finished. I embraced Falconer's criticism, allowed in her implicit rewriting, and duly cut the last line from all subsequent publications of 'Nhill'.)

But back to my story about a story: for it was only in my early forties (and again, oddly enough, with Falconer's help) that I realised that, besides what I thought I had been doing with 'Nhill' all those years, I was also engaging with the art-historical genre of the still life, and struggling, albeit unconsciously, with the transformation into writing, and into story, of a visual-arts mode – the still life – that is antagonistic to both writing and story.

It fascinates me that perhaps it was necessary to the process of writing 'Nhill' (which has now been published several times) *that I did not know* exactly what I was doing until well after I had done it. I believe that sometimes a writer's process can benefit from what I like to call a 'shaped unawareness' – simply put, a balance between what you know you are doing, and what you guess will only emerge later on, perhaps even many years later on (although funnily enough, a reader can sometimes see instantly what a writer might never see…).

In some ways, writers are always writing around – shaping themselves to – an absence that the very act of writing brings, quite mysteriously, into some sort of a presence. I say 'quite' mysteriously. I don't want to suggest that writing comes out of a place wholly inaccessible to rational analysis and/or to the interventions of writing teachers. Rather, to get to grips with this idea of writing's mystery, one needs to give the slip to those conventions of Western thinking that tend to banish anything not rational – not immediately open to engagement by the conscious mind – to a distant and frequently sneered-at domain of the (so-called) inscrutable, incomprehensible or unexplainable. (Sneered at by logical types, that is, but often loved too much by those artists who consider creativity something that you either have or you don't have, as if from birth.)

Eastern approaches such as Taoism offer a fruitful alternative to this 'either/or' logic of much (not all) Western thinking. Through such maxims as Wang Pi's 'learn not learn'[3] or 'he learns to be unlearned'[4], Taoism brings the irrational, the mysterious, to the very doorstep of the rational, the explicable. To this extent, the so-called mysterious process by which writing brings things to light that did not seem to be there before is not inexplicable at all.

The medium of writing – language – is in Julia Kristeva's striking titular term, an 'unknown'.[5] But what an 'unknown' it is! For don't we know it, use it, and observe its effects all the time? Creative writers need to walk the fuzzy line of this unknown/known distinction. To know writing better, its nuts and bolts, is at the same time to know its magic better. Itself, writing thus disrupts the largely Western hard-and-fast distinction between the known and the unknown.

(Incidentally, the little genealogical research that I have done into my own surname – 'West' – indicates that it would have been used to describe a person who had *come out of the West into the East*. True or not, I hold to this suggestion as a personal signifier of my own cross-cultural approach to creative writing.)

But back to 'Nhill'. A tiny phrase in Delia Falconer's review in *ABR* triggered the realisation that, on an unconscious level, I had been rewriting still life in my story. Falconer's description in her review of the 'oddly attentive landscape' of my story caught my eye because it reminded me of something that I had recently come across in a discussion of still life by Gilles Deleuze.[6] Deleuze characterises the still life as a 'presence and composition of objects which are wrapped up in themselves or become their own container'.[7] In this line of Deleuze's, I saw a connection to my story, as interpreted by Falconer, because an 'oddly attentive landscape' suggested to me a landscape that was somehow attending to itself, or as it were 'wrapped up in' itself or its 'own container'.

You might think this a leap too far – to most people, an 'oddly attentive landscape' would likely suggest, at least at first, a 'becoming character' or anthropomorphisation of the landscape rather than some art-historical notion – but when I went back to my story, for the umpteenth time as a writer and/or a reader, I wondered how the connection to still life could have remained so elusive to me down the years, even granted that my knowledge of still life was developing from off a very low base.

Still life is primarily a painterly genre, which Norman Bryson defines in terms of ordinary, everyday things: for example, 'bowls, jugs, pitchers and vases'.[8] Sometimes, still life extends beyond objects to include acts of etiquette or daily habit.

Bryson relates still life to the domain of 'low-plane reality': the realm of 'the small-scale, trivial, forgettable acts of bodily survival and self-maintenance'.[9] More technically, he also calls this the 'slowest, most entropic level of material existence'.[10]

By 'material', Bryson means that still life is woven through the 'local conditions' of history.[11] The fact that still life is so very *ordinary* in its choice of subjects, and relatedly, that it is 'the genre at the furthest remove from narrative', gives the false impression that it transcends history.[12] But for Bryson, the still life is more, not less, material in its involvement with everyday life (with the sub-strata of the very materiality of history).

In this way, then, still life severs the connection between history and narrative. It shows that history (material existence) can take place even – even especially – when no story, or at least no story of consequence, seems to be taking place.

This is where things start to get interesting for 'Nhill' as a story about still life, for the imperative of the short story (to express a narrative) apparently comes into conflict with the imperative of the still life (more analogous to, say, poetry) towards non-narrative, or anti-story.

The second element to our definition of still life (the first concerned its concentration on ordinary, everyday things as expressed by Bryson) helps refine this idea of still life as non-narrative. For still life has always, also, been associated with 'Vanitas'. Here, time also comes into it.

'Vanitas', according to Matilde Marcolli, is the portrayal of 'the transient nature of time, the fugitive instant, the brevity of life'.[13] Another name for this is 'memento mori'. The modest pleasures of still life – fresh flowers or a lavish meal – are tinged with the notion that all this will pass. The flowers have faded; the meal is over. Death eats away at the edges of life. 'Paintings in which fruit rots, flowers wither, insects nibble at leaves, and expensively set tables lie asunder served as a memento mori or *reminder of death*, intended to underscore life's transience and the greater weight of moral considerations'.[14]

Still life, then, is material in at least two senses: it possesses a material, everyday character of 'low-plane reality'; and it is enmeshed with the materiality of time's passage: 'Vanitas'.[15] In combination, how still-life objects 'are wrapped up in themselves or become their own container' might be read as a sign of everyday life taking shelter against time's onslaught.[16] Still life is a moment plucked precariously from eternity.

From one perspective, still life eschews grand narratives (its 'plot' is very minimal), but in another sense its story is the grandest of them all, for it concerns nothing less fundamental than our existence in time.

The eponymous town of Nhill is said to get its name from a corruption of an Aboriginal word 'nyell' meaning 'the abode of spirits'.[17] There is something going on here that links to 'Vanitas' and to time, but to me the strongest connection of my story to still life comes with the scene at the lake on pages 149–51.

Here, everything is 'wrapped up in [itself] or [becomes its] own container'.[18] Not to mention, everything is so still, so still-life-like. 'Across the lake we could see three waterbirds still as statues…' 'Reflections from the surface of the lake were mixed with the appearance of its bottom…' 'Nothing stirred…'

My story resonates particularly, I suggest, with Marcolli's description of the still life in the works of twentieth-century Italian painter Giorgio Morandi: 'In the absence of time… Space here is absolute stillness'.[19]

This might appear to contradict the theory of still life as a genre of time but in fact it doesn't. The gap between a moment of time and the eternity of time is an almost impossible distance: a space in which time must in some sense be absent.

Even though I came late to the idea of 'Nhill' as still life, recognising it as such, now, allows me to notice how, as an example of creative-arts practice, it speaks back to the art-historical notions of the genre.

Bryson sees almost no narrative in still life; Marcolli sees no time at all in Morandi. But my line 'a million days of evaporation' seems to relocate narrative and time *within the landscape itself*. Or rather, it suggests time's 'soaking up' into the level of narrative. Time, in a very raw sense granted, is present as narrative. In other words, 'Nhill', as a story that *must tell a story*, seems to take the time-based energies of still life and transform them into a narrative of deeply felt place.

I am not an Aboriginal writer, and I claim no special connection to Aboriginality. However, it is possible that, in noticing that 'Nhill' was always already a writing of still life before I knew it was, I am really only being alerted to its still earlier condition as a story: that is, to the at least 'a million days' of Aboriginal, spiritual occupation of the land, which registers what non-Aboriginal thinkers might call 'Vanitas'.

The challenge of experiencing, as a narrative, both eternity and a moment, which the Western still life flunks or evades, is re-clothed in both 'Nhill' and 'nyell' in Indigenous form.

You can never tell where writing will take you…

Endnotes

1. Moore, M 2013 'Baseball and Writing', at http://www.poets.org/viewmedia.php/prmMID/15658 (accessed 1 November 2013).

2. Falconer, D 2006 'Radical Drewe', *Australian Book Review*, rev. of *The Best Australian Stories 2006*, December 2006-January 2007, p44.

3. Chan, W-T 1969 *A Source Book in Chinese Philosophy*, Princeton University Press, Princeton, New Jersey, p170.

4. ibid.

5. Kristeva, J 1989 *Language: The Unknown: An Initiation into Linguistics*, Columbia University Press, New York.

6. Falconer, D loc. cit.

7. Deleuze, G 1989 *Cinema 2: The Time-Image*, Athlone Press, London, p16.

8. Bryson, N 1990 *Looking at the Overlooked: Four Essays on Still Life Painting*, Harvard University Press, Cambridge, Massachusetts, p13.

9. ibid., p14.

10. ibid., p13.

11. ibid., p12.

12. ibid., p9.

13. Marcolli, M 2013 'Still Life as a Model of Spacetime', at www.its.caltech.edu/~matilde/StillLifeSpacetime.pdf (accessed 14 January 2013), p4.

14. National Gallery of Art, Washington 2007 *Painting in the Dutch Golden Age: A Profile of the Seventeenth Century*, at http://www.nga.gov/content/dam/ngaweb/Education/learning-resources/teaching-packets/pdfs/dutch_painting.pdf (accessed 1 November 2013) p87.

15. Bryson, op. cit., p14.

16. Deleuze, loc. cit.

17. Van Der Putte, M 2004 'Climate of Nhill', at http://www.weather-climate.com/nhill.pdf (accessed 1 November 2013) p2.

18. Deleuze, loc. cit.

19. Marcolli, op. cit., p26.

'ARCHITECTURE'

Jennifer Mills

I have a layover in Shanghai for a night, which I mainly spend getting on and off the metro and walking, sweating in crowds, buffeted by warm bodies. I sleep in a pleasant, air-conditioned hotel room and leave mid-morning. The airport bus goes past the dead Expo site and I regret only catching glimpses of the space. My flight to Hohhot is uneventful, half full of silent businessmen and businesswomen, half empty.

I have no idea why Mr Wang has invited me to redesign his city. I am twenty-three, only a couple of years out of Honours. After an internship, I started my own company and have done a couple of renovation jobs for parents of friends, the odd work for the local council. I filled out the tender as an exercise, really. It was a surprise when contracts, visa forms and flight details began to arrive in my inbox.

*

When I get off the plane in Hohhot there is a man there to greet me, not Mr Wang but a man who works for him, and this man rolls my suitcase to a black car. 'Welcome, Miss Bourne,' the man says. His suit is not a uniform, but something about him gives me the impression he's a security guard. He smiles at my questions, but doesn't answer any of them as he drives me to the city.

The city is four hours from the capital. Four hours of empty grass plains, a lawn-ish wilderness that fades to brown and grey. When I look out at the plains I think about dust storms moving in, about desertification. The city isn't signposted. It has no name as yet.

We enter from an eight-lane overpass, sweep through some gracefully curved freeway exits, into the empty CBD. There is a good park with a lake. I can see swans, or maybe geese, floating there. They might be plastic. We pull up at the glass and brass of a five-star hotel, my accommodation for the duration of my contract. Mr Wang's employee doesn't get out of the car. A member of the hotel's staff takes my bags, pours tea, escorts me in the elevator to my suite on the eleventh floor. It has a good view over the curved urban streetscape. Between tall apartment buildings, I can see through to the fine symmetry of the surrounding city, and then beyond to its edges, where it dissolves into empty plains.

*

I applied for the job of building a city, but the city is already here. Actually, I am the thirteenth architect to come to work on the city as a whole, not counting the many others who have designed various individual buildings, parks and streets. Mr Wang insists it is not finished, though he tells me that his office is bombarded with enquiries from real estate investors every day. He isn't ready to sell anything just yet. He wants the place to be perfect. Billions are at stake. Perfecting it is in my hands. He makes this introductory speech over the phone shortly after I arrive and it turns out to be as voluble as he gets.

*

Initially I am daunted by the responsibility, but excited by the challenge too. I work long hours alone in the hotel room. When I am hungry I ring downstairs for sandwiches. That's all they have, sandwiches. In the evenings I Skype or Facebook my friends back home – the hotel has a foreign IP to dodge the firewall – or read up on feng shui and local weather patterns. Mr Wang calls me every Friday afternoon to check on my progress. I am very grateful to have this job, I tell him, expecting another speech.

'Australia,' he says. 'Good universities, good architects.'

*

I have the impression that Mr Wang is the director of a Hong Kong company with several government contracts for this kind of thing, or possibly a government official who orders such contracts from an office in Hong Kong, but I'm not sure and I don't ask. He almost always calls from Hong Kong. He doesn't seem to have many spare hours to fly up here. But given that he is in charge of so much future, he must be a Party official too. I don't enquire too deeply. From what I've read, relationships here are often vague.

*

When I need a break I walk around the empty streets, finding disconnects and flaws. There are some good buildings here, some exciting new work. There's an opera house in the shape of an egg with its top cracked off, a winding artificial river that culminates in the lake, an elegant mall set back in carefully cultivated gardens. Automated streetlights go on and off to guide my way. It is only a small city, intended for a population of about five million. Enough for a small public transport system – there is a fine elevated network of electric trains, which don't run yet, though I like the way the rail sweeps between the buildings. It is quite futuristic in design, even avant-garde in places, with a nod to the classical European styles of some of the buildings I saw in Shanghai. The integration could be better. There are a few Dutch-looking clock towers that should really go.

Back in the office that I have made out of one half of my suite, I pore over the plans. Since I don't read Chinese, I have had to ask for English versions to be made up for me. Until then I look at the overall patterns, the arches and circles, sort through the symmetries, trying to identify areas where the flow of the place might be perfected.

*

The English plans take a few weeks to arrive. My Friday conversations with Mr Wang are somewhat stilted; I am working fourteen-hour days, but I don't feel busy enough. When the concierge downstairs hands me the postal roll, I am happy, thinking my real work can now begin. Back upstairs, I take a can of coffee from the restocked fridge and open the roll.

The plans are identical, apart from the copy. I spread them out on my light box and set about transferring some of my ideas onto new sheets, tracing over the already duplicated cities. I sketch roughly at first and then concentrate on the finer details. When I do, I begin to notice that some of the names on the plans are familiar. There are signatures on several of the buildings. Curious, I start to look up some of the names. It seems the cracked-egg opera house was designed by someone I knew at university, a star student who transferred to the States in third year. It's an uncanny coincidence, I think. Then I see another familiar name. The artificial river was built by an engineering firm that belongs to my high school boyfriend's father. I believe he works there now, though we haven't spoken since we dated. And the elevated railway is by the woman who taught me Civil in third year. I eat a Snickers from the minibar and sleep on these coincidences.

*

On Friday afternoon the phone rings, and I answer it.

'Mr Wang, how are you?'

'Very good. How is my city?'

'Working hard,' I say. 'Mr Wang, I have a question.'

'Shoot,' he says.

'How did you choose me for this position?'

There is a nervous silence down the phone and for a minute I assume he is not going to answer the question at all. I listen to his breathing, oddly personal through the land line in a way that breaths never are through mobile phones.

'I mean, I don't have a lot of experience. How did you select me?' I say, in case he has not understood.

'Facebook,' he says.

'But how many applicants did you have?'

'You were the only one invited to tender,' he says.

Then Mr Wang explains his theory: 'There is an elite in each country. In Australia it is very small. So all the professionals are connected. We find you by looking at who you know. Every employer does this now,' he says. 'It doesn't matter what you have done, it matters to whom you belong.'

I want to tell him that I no longer belong to Damien, the high school boyfriend-engineer, or Dr Jahangir, the third-year Civil lecturer. But he interrupts my thoughts.

'I am coming down in a fortnight,' he says. 'To see your progress. Please be ready Friday.'

'Certainly, Mr Wang,' I say. He hangs up halfway through his own name.

*

I work extra hard over the following fortnight, though I get a bit distracted. I can't stop Googling the other people who have also worked on the city. Every time I look someone up I find there is some connection. Most of the urban shopping areas were designed by the company I did my internship with. The lake plantings were arranged through a horticulturalist friend of my uncle's, whose holiday house we used to stay in when we were kids. I suppose the architecture world is small, and Mr Wang says he can trust Australians. And those connected to us. After a while I stop finding it spooky and start to see this as part of my inevitable participation in the urban plan. A kind of fate.

*

Two weeks later, Mr Wang and I are driving around the empty city in a golf buggy. He is smaller and older than I imagined. He takes me on a tour of the golf course, part of a leisure complex designed by my former babysitter, who is now working for a sports science consultancy, more Googling revealed, which had secured a bunch of Olympics contracts. The place seems loosely based on the park she used to take me to when I was a kid, though that park has long since been turned into high-rise apartments. On closer inspection the element of memory is illusory, something I am projecting on to the place. It's entirely fresh, entirely itself.

We pull up by the lake. The geese, which are indeed real, scatter noisily into the water, making a rough scratch in the plane of perfect silence.

We return to my office, or to the office part of my suite. I am embarrassed by the bed, though the hotel staff have discreetly remade it in my absence.

'My suggestions,' I say as I show Mr Wang the unfurled plans.

'It is all fine, fine,' he says, barely glancing at them. He stands at the window adjusting his tie, then does something on an iPad.

'We will have another meeting in one month,' he says.

'Sure,' I say.

*

I work even harder, straining my eyes under fluorescent lamps to find the right redesigns that will iron out all the flaws I can find. The high school should be moved closer to the park, and the high-rise car park further away from the bus terminal. I make a fresh plan of the city, then another. Thoroughfares need to be connected to transport hubs. Railway lines need to intersect, not disappear.

After one month, I am convinced I have found every error, every potential accident blackspot and design flaw in the place. I am glad I have done so in time for Mr Wang's next visit.

'It is all going very well,' he says, leaning over my work. I feel proud, though I know he is only skim reading it.

'But really, Mr Wang, the city is fine already. It will work as it is. You could bring the people in. Start selling.'

'I know it is fine,' he says, calmly.

'Then why change it?' I say. I blush then, realising I might be talking myself out of six months' work.

'It is all here, but it's not perfect. It lacks something.'

I look down on the empty streets. 'The people?' I say.

'Not yet.'

*

So I go back to work. I have already solved all the significant issues I can find, but I keep looking for more. There is actually plenty to do, when I look for it. There are tiny improvements on every corner. Mr Wang won't send in construction teams until I am finished, and I am not finished until I say I am. But the following Friday, he calls to tell me we have to expand: homes for another five hundred thousand inhabitants. The local government has just approved it.

*

After another month I am tired of sourcing exactly the right kind of non-slip hand rail for the bus stop outside the retirement village, tired of replanting the park with low-allergenic, water-saving plants. I feel like I am almost ready and I think Mr Wang is too. Our Friday conversations are energised with this sense of urgency. But after several more weeks, I begin to get impatient.

'When are the people moving in?'

'Soon,' he says.

My next question is indelicate, so I begin it with: 'Sir, how much... Are there limits to what we can do here?'

'No,' he says. 'There are no limits. I am in rare earths. The region is monetising. We've even been green lighted to grow this project. We have a deeply motivated investment sector. They will wait.'

So he is a businessman, I think, if there is a distinction here.

'But rewiring the power underground for the new sector –' I say – 'it is going to cost a fortune.'

'There are many fortunes,' he says. 'More money than you can imagine.'

'Maybe that is the problem,' I say.

'I knew you had the vision to make the connections,' he says. 'I could see that from the beginning. Good network skills.' I can hear a slight agitation in his voice and I know that I have already asked too much.

'I mean, there is no problem,' I say. 'I will carry on.'

*

And I do, and it goes on. I order the redirection of special ribbed pavers at a major intersection to reduce trip hazards for the blind. I decide a small factory should be relocated half a mile north away from the wind range of a primary school. I redraw and redraw. But I am getting slower.

In the evenings, as I update my Facebook status with news on the various reconstructions, I start to think about what Mr Wang says about networks. I think about my friends – all young professionals who went to top-ranking schools – and whether we have a sense of ourselves outside our hundreds of friends and followers. The more elite friends I have, the stronger my sense of destiny. I look at the lists, think of the interests and connections we share. When I update my status I imagine how Mr Wang might see me from the outside. He probably sees me as more competent, more motivated and involved than I really am. I suppose that's how I want people to see me.

*

But even though my status updates remain enthusiastic, I start to get tired of the work. I grow bored with living in a hotel. With the permission of Mr Wang I move into an apartment building across the street; the staff come with me. On the inside, the apartment looks a bit like the home of a girl I played with when I was about ten, a girl named Brianna. Further searching reveals that she is now working as an interior designer: pictures of my new apartment are in her online portfolio. I realise I have stopped being surprised by this stuff.

The apartment building has a pool, and in my plans I quickly add one to the hotel. I spend long hours swimming laps. The water has the kind of silence I can bear. The pool is enormous, like the one we used for our high school swimming carnivals, and as I swim I imagine hundreds of girls in the stands, dressed in house colours, cheering me on.

I begin to sleep in, spend hours in front of karaoke dating shows on the flat screen, eating too many sandwiches. I go for long walks through the empty city and feed my crusts to the geese. I go entire days without working at all.

*

Mr Wang still calls me every Friday.

'We are close,' he says.

'Yes,' I say. 'Almost there.' I feel slightly annoyed.

'I am thinking about names,' he says. 'I am thinking about Simena. Ubar. Helike.'

'I like those,' I say.

'How are your designs going?'

I have done nothing for days. 'Well,' I say, 'I am still working on the bike paths. I can get a full plan to you later this week.'

'Take your time,' he says, 'I want everything to be perfect.'

'Okay,' I say.

'Also, we have the go-ahead for another industrial zone in the north-west.'

'Another one?'

'Another one.'

It will need workers, transport, retail zones, utilities. I sweep the chocolate bar wrappers from my desk and unroll a new sheet of paper. I begin to suspect that Mr Wang wants the city to stay empty. That we both do. With this thought I feel a shudder in my spine. I know I am going to be here forever. There is no function to this work except its destiny of growth, no purpose to my being here except as a prisoner.

After staring at the fresh sheet for a while, I ring downstairs to the concierge. There is a wave of static on the line and then a voice says, 'Miss Bourne, what would you like?'

'Listen,' I say in a low, urgent voice, 'what was here before?'

There is silence on the end of the line. Then a hushing sound, tinny and close. A machine.

'No past,' she says. 'Only future.'

I think about this for a moment. I lift the phone over my head to stretch my arm, then return it to my ear. When I return it the splashing static sound has cleared.

'Can I get a massage?' I say.

'Certainly.'

I scrunch up the blank sheet and reach for the remote control.

SURREAL PRIVILEGE

essay by Jennifer Mills

A story with this title should probably be more intentionally designed, but I rarely start with an idea about structure or form in mind. This story started, as most of mine do, with a nagging curiosity that swarmed around a particular image.

I went to China in 2010; I was lucky enough to be sent there on an Asialink residency. I did some travelling, but for the most part I was based in Beijing for two months, living in a little flat tacked above a hutong, writing on the roof in the smog, with the noise of construction ringing all around me. I went there with an interest in the rapid economic development and the social ramifications of all that progress. I was living in Alice Springs at the time, where mining has a huge impact on the landscape and people, and I wanted to see the other end of that resource chain.

While I was there I became fascinated by the phenomenon of ghost cities. The speed of development all over the country and the pace of urbanisation has led to the construction of whole cities well in advance of any population growth; some of these cities stand empty. People like to make photo-essays about them. Ordos is the most famous one, in Inner Mongolia. There is even a knock-off Disneyland ghost castle. Western media really enjoy being shocked by the excesses of Chinese construction, but it's actually very efficient in many ways – these enormous infrastructure projects just go up very quickly. I can't imagine Australia being half so good at high speed rail, for example. On the other hand, there's something very uncanny and a bit feudal about all those empty buildings, houses and hotels and shopping centres, waiting for migrant workers to become middle class.

I like the uncanny, especially in short stories. So I kept thinking about these ghost cities, and I wondered how that imagery might show up in a story, and how I might write my way into it in a way that didn't just reiterate the 'bad China'/'weird China' narratives so prevalent in the media.

I can't find the first draft of 'Architecture'. It's possible it's one of the few stories I started on screen. I usually write my first drafts longhand in cheap exercise books, because it's tactile, there's a natural pace to it. Also it's more pleasant and less work-like to write in a comfortable chair, rather than sitting at a desk in front of a laptop. Working on screen makes me edit, and makes me consider my audience, neither of which is very useful for a first draft. Sometimes this policy can backfire; for example, when I'm transcribing the whole first draft of a novel and I realise it's rubbish, but mostly it works for me. I usually only write enough to get a handle on the story, maybe about five hundred words, just until the wind goes out of my sails. Then I'll put it away for a week or two and come back to it. Very rarely I'll sit down and write an entire story from start to finish, and when this happens it's an enormous rush.

I think the first sentence I wrote was 'I have no idea why Mr Wang has invited me to redesign his city', which is not a good opening, but it became my premise, and it's what made me able to think about those images as a story. I added the preamble of Miss Bourne's arrival later, so that the reader arrives in the story and the city along with her. A young Australian architect seemed like an interesting way to approach the city, someone involved in the process of creating it, but not in charge.

As I wrote, I began to realise that it was really quite a strange situation. This woman's not sure why she's there; she has work to do, but gets increasingly lazy because of the apparent pointlessness of her work; and this mysterious Mr Wang character comes and goes, sometimes sinister, sometimes friendly, and talking in a lot of business jargon. While writing, I began to speculate: what if the city won't ever be finished? What if Miss Bourne begins to feel like a prisoner there? How would she respond?

It was only about two-thirds of the way through writing it that I realised what the story was really about, and where the metaphorical power of the empty city lay, and that was when Miss Bourne started to do what any normal twenty-three year old in unsupervised contract employment would do, which is spend all her time on Facebook. I realised that all this empty architecture was really a metaphor for social class and the shape of social networks, particularly the way that social networks can replicate elite privilege online. The way that class can be a trap.

After that, I had the story cornered. Mr Wang was able to explain his reasons for choosing Miss Bourne for the role: 'We find you by looking at who you know... It doesn't matter what you have done, it matters to whom you belong.' Later, she thinks of her online self as a fiction, but an elite fiction: 'He probably sees me as more competent, more motivated and involved than I really am. I suppose that's how I want people to see me.'

But at the same time as she realises this, her work begins to slacken; she becomes lazy, almost paralysed, and slowly realises that the city is a kind of infinite labour (I think I must have been reading a bit of Borges). She gradually becomes aware that the city will never be finished. There is no escape from the march of progress, and yet it's quite pointless. In the final scene, Miss Bourne more or less surrenders to her condition. It was in writing the end of this story, when she rings downstairs to the front desk, that I remember thinking of the title.

After I'd written the ending and figured out the ideas in it, then I went back and started to tidy and structure the story around those ideas. Form follows content, for me. I need to write the story to figure out what it's about, and then rewrite it with that in mind. Some images arise spontaneously – the geese, the imaginary school sports carnival cheering her as she swims – but some are inserted at this later stage, such as Mr Wang's suggestions for names for his city, which are all the names of lost historical cities (I visited Simena by boat in 2005).

Writing in China required care. The cliché isn't just a feature of language, but of thought. As a white writer I have to guard against the patterns of privilege in my own thinking, beware of reiterating stereotypes (such as the inscrutable Chinese man). We all dwell in the architecture of privilege. I wanted to write Mr Wang as a real businessman, a person, and so I was careful to make his dialogue articulate a consistent, if slightly sinister, world view. I wanted the city to be a specific place, not the 'weird China' my Australian imagination can so easily access. I'm not sure how well I succeeded, but it's always something I find I struggle against. Being in this ridiculously fortunate situation where Asialink had sent me off to China to look around I was very conscious of this, and as I found myself trying to explain the concept of arts grants and overseas residencies to Chinese people without much success, I was constantly reminded of the surreal privilege of being able to work internationally. At the same time, being in a foreign place where you don't speak the language is a good way to shock you out of taking that access for granted.

For me, writing and reading is a cheap way of travelling. I love the experience of being other people. It's never complete, of course, but I think that the transformative capacity of the imagination is nothing short of magic, and it keeps me returning to fiction despite the problems of making a living and the sometimes exhausting effort of pulling worlds from the air. But that kind of imaginative mobility has to be learnt, and it comes with a great deal of responsibility.

The storyteller has a cultural responsibility, but to which culture? I think there is a tendency, especially in Australia, to use a lot of collective terms – 'we' 'us' – for what is in fact a specific experience, often of straight white males. Fiction returns that specificity to a human experience – it is always a political act. But I am very conscious of what kind of meaning I am trying to make, whose story I am telling and why. I try to be conscious of my privilege in a way that doesn't result in silence or paralysis. Architecture is about that struggle too.

Of course, being in China only two months, no amount of reading and talking to people and self-consciousness could make up for my *laowai* ignorance, and I couldn't easily slip into a Chinese person's thoughts, certainly not with the little understanding of the language I had (I could probably slip into a dumpling's thoughts, in a pinch). In approaching the stories that I wrote in China, I found myself working towards a sense of place and a specific experience that was also bound up in my being an outsider there.

Many of the stories in my first collection travel – from all over Australia to Mexico, the USA, Russia – but in many of these I am really interested in the absurdity and strange anxiety of whiteness. Whiteness isn't something I can escape through fiction but it's certainly something I can make fun of, draw out, and challenge.

My short stories tend to go in for weirdness. When I try to address the specific and the human, I always seem to end up finding my way to the magical, the alien, or the surreal. 'Architecture' is an example of this – the situation seemed surreal already, and only required a slight adjustment to become vaguely dystopian. That quality of vagueness is important to me, and I try to use it sparingly. To me, the best short fiction hovers in an ambiguity. It is the tension of holding that ambiguity, that internal contradiction – what Keats called 'negative capability' – that gives the form its power. The stories I love the most don't explain themselves. They just let strange things happen.

As I am also a novelist, I find this quality of short fiction immensely refreshing and exciting to play with. It encourages spontaneity and lightness, untetheredness – choosing the title *The Rest is Weight* for my collection was a nod to this pleasure. On the other hand, the surreal could probably be a burden if it became schtick. Writers like Etgar Keret and George Saunders seem to be able to enter these parallel worlds with ease, but I sometimes wonder if they feel typecast, fixed in a certain expected mode. Publishing can bring on all of these anxieties, and it's probably best to ignore that side of things as much as possible and just do whatever interests you. Following my curiosity is how I ended up reading and then writing, so I'm not about to alter that strategy.

The experience of the surreal is in some ways quite natural to me. I am attracted to people and experiences that are reality-liminal. I'm very interested in neurodiversity and different ways of experiencing perception. Conflicting realities can cause social conflict, too, so I guess that brings me back to politics. Just look at climate change, where there is a section of the population that science will never convince. The same goes for religion. Human beings are mostly insane.

Probably my earlier stories exhibit the beginnings of this tendency. 'Architecture' is one of the later stories in this first collection, which spans about five years of writing. Its surreality points in a direction I'm pursuing, but I also want to be careful about that. I'm hesitant with words like 'surreal' or 'magical realism' because those seem like pretty rigid categories. I work across genres, and trying to become more flexible as a writer is important to me.

I call what I'm doing work most of the time but I'm happiest when I'm just tooling around. That's the payoff for me, getting to muck around in the ideas. Not every day is fun, but enough of them are that I still feel, more than a decade into my so-called career, that I am incredibly lucky to be getting away with something so unusual.

ACKNOWLEDGEMENTS

Michael Wilding's quote from *Wild & Woolley, A Memoir* used with permission from Giramondo.

'An Australian Short Story', Ryan O'Neill, *The Lifted Brow*, Issue 14.

'Nhill', Patrick West, *The World Swimmers*, Perth: The International Centre for Landscape and Language for CREATEC at Edith Cowan University, 2011, pp1-8.

'Three Sisters', Maria Takolander, *The Double*, Text Publishing, Melbourne, 2013.

'Twilight in Caeli-Amur', Rjurik Davidson, *Dreaming Again*, Jack Dann (ed.), Voyager, Sydney, 2008.

'Architecture', Jennifer Mills, *The Rest is Weight*, UQP, 2012.

EDITORS

JULIE CHEVALIER lives in Sydney. *Permission to Lie*, a collection of her short stories, was published by Spineless Wonders in 2011. Her most recent poetry collection, *Darger: his girls* (Puncher & Wattmann, 2012) won the Alec Bolton prize for an unpublished poetry manuscript and was short-listed for the WA Premier's Poetry Prize.

She has a BA (English with teaching qualifications, St Lawrence University, USA), a MA (Literature from the University of Sydney), and a MA (Writing by Research, University of Technology, Sydney). She has extensive experience teaching teenagers and adults, and writing educational resources.

She co-edited *Small Wonder* and *Stoned Crows*, anthologies of prose poems and microfiction.

BRONWYN MEHAN is the founding publisher of Spineless Wonders. Her short fiction and poetry have been published in *The Age* newspaper and various literary journals. She has post-graduate qualifications in communications, professional and creative writing and an MA in Linguistics (University of Technology, Sydney).

A former Head Teacher, English, Bronwyn has taught in New South Wales high schools and TAFE and is a former member of the School and Higher School Certificate Syllabus Committees. She has worked as a freelance editor and creative writing teacher in NSW and the Northern Territory.

CONTRIBUTORS

CLAIRE AMAN lives in Grafton, NSW. She works as a town planner and writes in her spare time. Her short stories have been published in *Best Australian Stories* (Black Inc), *New Australian Stories 1* and 2 (Scribe), *Escape* (Spineless Wonders), *Australian Book Review*, Island, *Southerly*, *Heat*, *Griffith Review*, and read on ABC Radio. She won the *Wet Ink* short story prize in 2013, and the EJ Brady and Hal Porter short story prizes in 2014. Her writing life has been nurtured at Varuna and through an Australian Society of Authors mentorship.

TONY BIRCH's books include *Shadowboxing* (Scribe, 2006), *Father's Day* (Hunter, 2009) and *Blood* (UQP, 2011), shortlisted for the Miles Franklin award (2012). *The Promise*, a collection of stories, will be released in 2014. Tony teaches at the University of Melbourne and works with community groups. He lives in Carlton, just around the corner from where he was born.

RJURIK DAVIDSON is Associate Editor of *Overland* magazine and the author of *The Library of Forgotten Books* (PS Publishing, 2010) and *Unwrapped Sky* (Tor, 2014). He lives in Melbourne. rjurik.com

MICHAEL GIACOMETTI's writing illuminates the experience of suffering that is this worldly life. He has won several competitions and his work is featured in *Meanjin*, *Island*, and print and online anthologies including *Escape* (Spineless Wonders, 2011) and *The Inland Sea* (Ptilotus Press, 2013). He is currently writing an outback-gothic novel, *This landscape of failure*, with the support of an ArtsNT grant. He lives in Alice Springs.

MARION HALLIGAN was born in Newcastle and grew up by the sea. She has now published some twenty books and has written short stories, articles, book reviews and essays for various publications. She believes fiction illuminates our lives, and for this reason she loves to read it as well as write it. Her most recent book is a collection of short stories, *Shooting the Fox* (Allen & Unwin, 2011).

ANDY KISSANE's book of short stories, *The Swarm* (Puncher & Wattmann, 2012), was longlisted for the Frank O'Connor International Short Story Award. He is the Coriole National Wine Poet and six of his poems are featured on the back of Coriole's Cabernet Shiraz. His latest collection of poetry is *Radiance* (Puncher & Wattmann, 2014). andykissane.com

JENNIFER MILLS is the author of two novels, *Gone* and *The Diamond Anchor*, and a collection of short stories, *The Rest is Weight* (all published by UQP). Her work has received wide critical acclaim and won numerous awards both nationally and internationally. In 2012 she was named a *Sydney Morning Herald* Best Young Australian novelist. She is currently the fiction editor at *Overland*. Find her at jenjen.com.au and @millsjenjen.

RYAN O'NEILL was born in Glasgow in 1975. He lived in Africa, Europe and Asia before settling in Newcastle with his wife and two daughters. His work has appeared in numerous journals and anthologies, and he has been shortlisted for the Queensland Literary Awards and the NSW Premier's Literary Awards. He teaches at the University of Newcastle. His collection, *The Weight of a Human Heart*, was published by Black Inc in 2012.

MARIA TAKOLANDER is the author of a book of short stories, *The Double* (Text, 2013); two poetry collections, *Ghostly Subjects* (Salt, 2009) and *The End of the World* (Giramondo, 2014); and a scholarly book, *Catching Butterflies: Bringing Magical Realism to Ground* (Peter Lang, 2007). She is a Senior Lecturer in Literary Studies and Professional and Creative Writing at Deakin University in Geelong, Victoria.

PATRICK WEST is a Senior Lecturer in Professional and Creative Writing at Deakin University and author of *The World Swimmers* (Edith Cowan University, 2011). In 2012, Patrick wrote and co-produced the 27-minute fictional-documentary film *Sisters of the Sun* (directed by Simon Wilmot). He co-edited, with Om Prakash Dwivedi, *The World To Come* (Spineless Wonders, 2014).

MORE BOOKS FROM SPINELESS WONDERS

SINGLE AUTHOR

In this eclectic collection, O'Flynn, an accomplished poet, turns his hand to linked short stories, micro-fiction and monologues.

'O'Flynn's faultless ear for laconic Aussie parlance, his wry ability to turn a story in a moment from comedy to tragedy and back again, his exhilaratingly deft range...all this makes him one of a kind, in my opinion. A hugely enjoyable collection.'
CATE KENNEDY

In this short story collection, travellers on highways and trains are preoccupied with the lives of the dead, with lost children or with parents. A woman searches a suburban deadland for her missing mother. A rural family struggles on a land that fails to sustain them. A young man's attempt to leave the strictures of family life ends in violence.

'A talent to watch.'
WALTER MASON

In these seventeen stories, Melbourne writer, Mary Manning, looks at the ways people are shaped, or damaged, by their circumstances. The results may sometimes be humorous, sometimes tragic. Whether set on a tram, along a highway or on an outback road – it is the journey, the characters and the telling of the tale that will capture your attention.

'Tart, tight and compulsively readable.'
PADDY O'REILLY

COLLECTIONS

What makes a man? In this collection of short stories, Pierz Newton John moves through the full range of masculine experience. He is not afraid to show men as lonely, sexual, loving, sometimes vulnerable, sometimes abusive.

'A startling collection...sly humour and memorable characters.'
CHRIS WOMERSLEY

This entertaining collection includes a romp of a novella as well as short stories and micro fictions all set in and around contemporary Melbourne. Sometimes serious, sometimes seriously playful – always written in breathtakingly beautiful prose.

'A writer of sharp originality who must be taken seriously.'
VANESSA GEBBIE

In *Permission to Lie*, Julie Chevalier casts a curious eye into many different worlds. Her characters ride the citybound bus route, spend the night in a nudist colony and wait tables. Quirky and beautifully-written, these stories provide insights that ring with integrity and compassion.

'A new voice in Australian fiction, wry, gritty, knowing and true.'
FIONA MCGREGOR

SHORT FICTION ANTHOLOGIES

In this anthology, we pay tribute to the undeniable cultural influence that American TV programs such as Twilight Zone and Outer Limits have had on our lives 'down under'. 'These TV dramas,' says editor, Angela Meyer, 'were often metaphors for equality, justice, the nuclear threat and more. Though they were just as often pure, spooky fun.'

'A disturbing and thought-provoking collection.'
ADELAIDE REVIEW

If you like your genres with a bit of edge, you'll love this diverse collection of stories from Spineless Wonders. Features award-winning writers Ryan O'Neill, Jen Mills, Andy Kissane, Louise Swinn, Julie Chevalier, A.S. Patrić and Kim Westwood as well as stories chosen by Sophie Cunningham in the inaugural Carmel Bird Short Fiction Award.

'Quality short fiction, packed with surprises. Prepare to be transported.'
MARION HALLIGAN

The *Carmel Bird* Award

PROSE POEMS & MICROFICTION ANTHOLOGIES

What do our best wordsmiths have to say about Australian icons? This anthology takes a fresh look at everything from the HIH collapse to crocs, Margaret Olley, bush burials and the ABC. We visit a post-apocalyptic Opera House and spend Saturday night in downtown Byron Bay.

'A celebration of the many things Australia can mean to us.'
NEWTOWN REVIEW OF BOOKS

Here are short and clever pieces by thirty contemporary Australian writers on topics ranging from the eroticism of mash potato, parenting as magic realism and a tongue-in-cheek history of the Cyclops bicycle. Includes award-winning writers Michael Farrell, Keri Glastonbury, Judith Beveridge, Peter Boyle, Kent MacCarter, Erin Gough and Charles D'Anastasi.

'A treasure trove.' READINGS MONTHLY

The *joanne burns* Award

BOOKS ON WRITING

Dear Writer Revisited, a book about writing and the imagination, is now re-released with new material and updated advice for the twenty-first century writer.

"Carmel Bird has updated her brilliant guide to those who are perplexed by writing. *Dear Writer Revisited* is a dazzling, humane and witty book which will be enlightening for anyone who picks it up, however experienced she or he may be. This is a classic account of how to write. I know of nothing that equals it."

PETER CRAVEN

'I first read *Dear Writer* as a nervy, secretive scribbler-in-journals 20 years ago. Reading this revised version I'm struck again by its practical generosity on technical matters - but am also inspired by the deeper, more complex conversations I think I missed in those early readings: about courage, about the urgency and mystery and self-discovery of the writing process. *Dear Writer Revisited* may masquerade – convincingly – as a book for beginners, but its lessons are mature and wise.'

– CHARLOTTE WOOD

THE WRITER'S ROOM INTERVIEWS

EARWORMS

Earworms are those songs with unforgettable hooks that get stuck in your head but Spineless Wonders brings you short Australian earworms – stories by award-winning writers that you definitely won't want to forget.

Stuck in a queue? Don't stress. You can listen to our selection of funny, political and thought-provoking prose poems and microfiction from our anthologies, *Small Wonder* or *Stoned Crows.*

Got a pile of washing-up or ironing to do? Housework's not a chore when you can listen to short fiction from our anthologies, *Escape* or *The Great Unknown.*

Commuting every day? Traffic jams are not a problem when you can listen to the latest in contemporary Australian short fiction from Spineless Wonders.

Prices range from $0.99 to $2.99. Gift vouchers available. Listen to our audio trailers at

www.shortaustralianstories.com.au/audio

NOTES

NOTES

www.ingramcontent.com/pod-product-compliance
Lightning Source LLC
Chambersburg PA
CBHW031237210726
48287CB00003B/806

9781925052039